SPARROW
# nights

David GILMOUR

COUNTERPOINT
WASHINGTON, D.C.

Copyright © 2002 by David Gilmour

First Published in 2001 by Random House Canada

Library of Congress Cataloging-in-Publication Data
A CIP catalog record for this book is available from the Library of Congress

ISBN 1-58243-203-1

FIRST PRINTING

COUNTERPOINT
P.O. Box 65793
Washington, D.C. 20035-5793

Counterpoint is a member of the Perseus Books Group

10 9 8 7 6 5 4 3 2 1

for JESSE GILMOUR

I cannot get used to things that end.

— MARCEL PROUST
*in a letter to a friend*

CHAPTER 1

Let me come back, just for a second, to Emma Carpenter. She had been introduced by the chairman at a cocktail party and I thought, there's something wrong with her. She smells funny. Indeed she did, a kind of acrid odour, like a frightened animal, and it seemed very odd to me that such a sophisticated young woman would turn up at a gathering of professionals, smelling.

Later, when she was gone, I made a casual observation to a colleague, a Frenchman, who claimed not to have noticed anything at all. But then again, Serrault is always claiming not to understand the obvious. I think he fancies it makes him seem more complicated than the rest of us. And it does, of course.

I knew very little about her actually, and I tried to keep it that way. For all the modesty of my professional accomplishments, my failings at marriage, my childless life, the faded-away friendships, in spite of all these things, I was quite a happy man and I didn't need a mess. I observed, however, that she wore black, rather cheap running shoes to class; that she had waited two years before applying to graduate school. I have no idea what she did in the meantime; probably a great deal of sex; there was something of that in her, a kind of propriety which, one suspected, protects a pornographic imagination. I don't know. Perhaps in saying that, I am revealing more about myself than her.

I can tell you something else about Emma, since you've got me gossiping. As a favour to Serrault, to whom she had been assigned, I read a number of her undergraduate papers. They were perfectly satisfactory, but she was brighter in person than on paper. Something froze in her when she "wrote," a ball of ice that appeared to melt almost entirely in conversation, where she could be shockingly direct. More about that later. She also had a surprising talent for mimesis. One day, in an unguarded moment, I overheard her referring to a conversation that had taken place the day before in the faculty lounge. A professor of linguistics had been going on and on, the way they do, and in recapping his remarks she had allowed herself a small imitation of his voice, which was like a door that needs oil. She delivered his nasal creak with such aplomb, to such a degree of perfection, that for a second the man in question seemed to materialize in front of us. What an effect it had! It was as if she had suddenly broken into fluent Arabic. It implied, this little party trick of hers, the presence of alien creatures within her slender frame, a notion that I found alarmingly erotic. But I didn't pursue her. By fifty-one I had learned the hard way that slim attractive young women . . . Well, why go into it. You know perfectly well what I'm saying. Besides, I had other problems.

For example, one fall day I was sitting in my study. It was a beautiful day and I'd left the back door open. You could smell autumn in the garden, the scent of the leaves, the cool air so sweet, so beyond-this-world. It was as if in the fragrance alone I could possess again the finest, most elusive sensations of my childhood, the clarity of things felt and seen and smelt and heard—a bird singing in the yard, a schoolboy's mechanical recitation: *porto, portas, portat*.

A yellow cat wandered in, purring and drooling and rubbing against my leg. I was writing a course description for the next year's calendar when I heard a strange sound, an irregular pop like a cap pistol. *Pop, pop*. Then silence. Then *pop*. But no, it wasn't a child's toy, it was something else. For some reason it amused me to guess what it was, and I stopped working and listened carefully. It didn't sound metallic, it sounded rather like . . . I couldn't put my finger on it, but I'd heard it before. But somewhere else, in an entirely different framing. It belonged back there with the vivid garden smells. But what could it be?

Finally, I went to see. Opposite my back patio, across a narrow lawn and a screen of rose bushes, stood a ragged flagpole on the next property. For some reason the tenant had raised a German flag. I'm not partial to Germans (although I rather like the sound of a woman speaking the language softly), but that's not the issue. The issue was the flag flapping. It snapped, it cracked in the wind. Abruptly

I recalled where I'd heard it: at summer camp. Late in the after-noons, limp from the sun and swimming, I used to lie on the dock, the drops of water falling from my brown skin. They made stains on the sun-bleached wood like little countries on a map. Closing my eyes, I would listen to the sound of the waves lapping under the dock, the sound of a motorboat across the bay—and a flag flapping overhead. But I didn't remember it being so loud. This was like a starter's pistol. *Crack, crack, crack.*

I went back to my study and resumed work, but once you notice something like that, after a while it's *all* you notice. Gradually my typing disintegrated, a sure sign I don't like what I'm writing, that my body is fighting it. Really, what a racket! Finally I surrendered and went for a closer look. I walked around the block and stood in front of the offending property. The sunshine was dazzling. I stared at the front parlour hoping by the intensity of my feelings to bring its owner to the window, as one can sometimes awake a sleeper by resting one's eyes on him for a protracted length of time. A stocky woman passed me on the sidewalk, a dog trotting at her side. Possibly a poor selection, but I looked to her as an ally. She nodded politely, deferring to my age I assume, but the *reason* I smiled at her didn't register, distracted as she was by the log-dumping hound that bounced empty-headedly beside her. My stomach began to ache; acid dripped like the inside of a sweating cave. This was intolerable. Too many provocations. But what could I do? How do you tell someone to take down his flag? Especially a German. Since the collapse of the Wall and the creation of their own army, I've noticed a new emphasis on civil liberties, *chez eux*. One always knows where that leads. I could send a note, but I've learned that anyone considerate enough to be touched by such a gesture has generally nosed out the problem beforehand. So I decided simply to take care of the business myself.

A kind of calm came over me like those delicious moments in bed when you can feel a sleeping pill coming on. I worked the rest of the afternoon unbothered by the flapping—unbothered because I knew it had a finite lifespan. I wondered if I could trick myself into never hearing the flag by constantly pretending to be on the verge of cutting it down. But when I was awoken from my nap by the *whack, whack, whack* from my neighbour's house—really, it sounded like a helicopter pad back there—I realized I'd been indulging in impotent philosophizing.

I went to dinner at my regular neighbourhood restaurant. I hesitated before ordering the mushroom risotto—I wanted to lose eight pounds in the event I met someone—but I went ahead anyway, assuming the adrenaline from the night ahead would burn it off. I treated myself to an expensive bottle of red wine, an American Cabernet, complex and elegant. After a glass I felt a comforting warmth as if I were no longer alone, as if a soft light had switched on inside me and was keeping me company.

I set the alarm for three in the morning, but I needn't have. A light wind blew off the lake and after the second or third pop of my neighbour's flag my eyes opened and I was wide awake. I sprang out of bed like a student on the first day of summer vacation. For a second I understood *in my blood* the lure of crime, its focus and clarity.

I thought perhaps I should go back and give Dostoevsky another go. So overwritten, so talkative, like a Methedrine addict. But still, he was on to something. I went about my preparations with automatic precision. I showered and shaved. I brushed my teeth and gargled vigorously just in case I was arrested. I laid out a selection of knives: a paring knife, a steak knife. But they dissatisfied me and I went into a bottom drawer and fetched a rusting carpet cutter. Everything was so clear; the kitchen danced with light. (I really *must* give *Crime and Punishment* another whirl.) I turned on the radio, a Schubert piano sonata, I think, but it intruded on my thoughts. Silence again fell over the kitchen.

I turned out the light and after a moment's pause I slipped into my backyard. A cricket stirred in the hedges. I opened the fence gate. I measured the steps to the flagpole in my head: one, two, three, four, five, up to eleven. I found the carpet cutter in my pocket, the metal sort of soapy-feeling. I slid the blade forward, the silence around me so complete you could hear the absence of sound. I took a series of rapid steps across the grass, slashed the rope with one stroke and left the flag floating like a corpse in the swimming pool.

CHAPTER 2

When I say my career has gone very well, I mean of course within certain restrictions, the principal one being a rather low ceiling on my ambition. I've always been attracted to university campuses. I remember once as an undergraduate visiting the office of a French professor where I observed, indeed I *inhaled* (because I could smell them), shelf after shelf of books. How mysterious they were, how I desired the "it" I knew they contained. A dictionary of *ancien français* lay open on the floor; his work desk was a shuffle of papers with small, confident notations in the margins. How happy I would be, I thought, if only I had such an office to go to every day. To belong to a room like this—imagine.

It was more *that* really than an infatuation with ideas or an interest in exchanging them that drew me into this world. From my first day I loved university life and I never wanted to leave it. Indeed I haven't.

I planned initially on a degree in English literature, but during my first year I fell in love with a tall, frizzy-haired philosophy student, Raissa Shestatsky. It was my first physical relationship and, my heavens, what a time I had of it, a blanket nailed over the window to keep out the sunlight, a swollen candle by the bed, the air thick with cigarette smoke and that raspberry incense she adored. In the afternoons we escaped the student cafeteria and came home to my flat and sometimes didn't emerge for days. And yet how used to it one became too, and so quickly, the breathtaking sexual availability of a lovely young woman. As if one had a divine right to it.

But she was an adventuress, my Raissa. A young man of my era, perhaps any era, could never imagine a girl being like that. She had a quick appetite for the world, of which I was only a single morsel, and riding my bicycle to an early Chaucer seminar one morning I spotted her in the doorway of an apartment building. You can presume what happened next: the tearful interrogation, the galloping heart, the sweat-soaked sheets, the masochistic imaginings. I lost twenty pounds; I didn't sleep, it seemed, for weeks on end. I smoked cigarettes and wept in the dark until I saw on the notice board an opening for students to study French language and literature at the University of Toulouse, four hundred miles south of Paris.

I signed up as if it were the Foreign Legion. But travel is never the escape one imagines. Quite the reverse, actually. By changing the landscape, one succeeds only in highlighting the familiar—in my case, a broken heart. Foolishly or heroically, I'm still not sure, I went daily to the poste restante to see if there was a letter from Miss

Shestatsky. Often there was. Now that I was out of the country, it was safe to love me again. Once there was attached a black-and-white photograph of her, a stunning picture: she was sprawled in a beanbag chair, long-limbed and inviting. In a rush of emotion I showed it to the postal clerk, who asked me if it was my wife, and, my ears going hot, I said yes it was. From that day on, whenever I picked up my mail, he would flip energetically through the stack of brightly stamped letters saying, "Let's hope there's something from your lovely wife, eh?" Ah yes, *ma belle femme*. It shamed me and pleased me at the same time, although I had a sensation in my blood cells that she was gone for good, up to God knows what cunnilingual atrocities.

It was a grim patch indeed, a cold winter, the streets wind-whipped and empty. I must have imagined I was having some sort of literary adventure, that my friends at home were reading my letters aloud to each other and pouring over a map of France as if I were a character in a novel. I imagined Raissa hearing stories about me, rueing the day she'd betrayed me. But I was very lonely and when I'm lonely I can't sleep, although the years have diminished that. Mostly I stayed awake till dawn, writing letters in an all night restaurant near the train yards. I can still see the snow shifting like lace over the railway tracks as I trudged home at daybreak. By the end I spoke quite good French. I talked to everyone, train workers, taxi drivers, crazy men, prostitutes, policemen, waiters, soldiers.

I had a little apartment near the university, a two-floor walk-up, and for a while a Spanish roommate, but we quarrelled about the gas bill and he moved out, insulted. So I was left to myself and my books. Exhausted from a night's writing, the cold and talking to myself, I crawled into bed and read plays. I assumed it was the best way to learn the spoken language. (I realize now it would have been better to read comic books and watch a lot of television, but my snobbery, my sense of letting down my audience, wouldn't permit that.) Near seven on those slate grey mornings a train chugged by my apartment window, cueing a profound sleep. It was as if I had been drugged. I turned off the light and smoked a final cigarette, staring up at the ceiling, returning to Raissa and a little room on Huron Street where I had made love to her one afternoon with her shirt still on.

It was dark when I awoke, always. While I still tell people I studied at the University of Toulouse, the truth is I attended very few classes. I couldn't get out of bed until the six o'clock evening train hurtled past my window. Shivering, I descended into the street and quickly covered the block and a half to a *boulangerie,* where I bought my evening meal. Even then I was a creature locked in habit. Two eggs, a slice of ham, a *petit* loaf of bread and a package of Gitanes. The blue pack with the swirling gypsy. Perhaps she'd been sampling the product herself: the cigarettes were so strong that sometimes I had to lie down, overcome with nausea and toxicity.

It might have been better if my French had been a little more ragged. It distressed me to see some gaudy American student, freshly arrived in town, walking hither and yon with a pretty French girl while she practised her execrable English. It seemed rather unfair.

But the person who commands the language commands the moment; I should have realized that sooner. As it was, I was relegated to the status of a well-meaning but rather dull foreigner, better than an Arab, but just. I met a girl at a student café on New Year's Eve who took me to midnight mass and then back to her olive-scented room. But when I returned two nights later, I could see through the shutters a candle burning inside and, standing stock-still, I heard—over the beat of my heart—the sound of intimate murmurings *là-dedans*!

Finally my sentence was up and I came home on a Russian ship. I phoned Raissa from a friend's house and we made a rendezvous for that evening. She turned up in a baggy turtleneck sweater and blue jeans. She'd had enough of philosophy, she claimed, and she started to tell me why when suddenly, out of nowhere, I yawned. I think it surprised us both. Somewhere in those amblings through dead-of-night Toulouse she had dried up in my heart and blown away. I was free.

CHAPTER 3

It must have been almost five years ago now, perhaps even to the day. I found myself standing in the middle of my living room. It was twilight, that rather sad time when curtains are drawn and the question *what shall I do* poses itself with unusual poignancy. I'd gotten up from the chesterfield and suddenly I couldn't think what to do next. I don't mean for the rest of my life or the next few years or for my summer vacation or for tomorrow's seminar—I mean for *that moment*. I could go over to the window and look out; I could go back to the chesterfield; go out for dinner; turn on the television. But each choice seemed equally stale and unsatisfying. It was like looking... let me explain this properly. You may have noticed that, at the onset of winter, city dwellers cover the shrubs on their lawns with burlap sacks to protect them from the ice and hail. Viewed at twilight, just before the street lamps go on, these shapes acquire a kind of baggy sameness. Standing in the middle of my living room, rocking slightly on the balls of my feet, I saw the upcoming events in my life rather like these vague silhouettes on a cold evening. All slightly different but essentially the same. Indeed for some time I had had the impression that people saw *me* as one of those bagged shrubs.

For some time after that I had the distinct impression that the light was slipping, stealing out of my life, that the days were growing shorter and shorter. I got up, I had breakfast, I walked to the university, bantered with a colleague, gave a lecture, came home, napped, and when I awoke, the day was over. It occurred to me with surprising neutrality that I was dying, that I had already lived my life but my heart was still beating as if it hadn't quite got the message.

I went for a walk, drawn by the idea of lights and bustle on Bloor Street, but it was dinnertime, a lull in the activity of a main street, and I wandered toward the heart of the city, thinking *What am I going to do? What?* I had gone as far as Yonge Street and had turned south when I saw Emma Carpenter. She was standing in front of a movie theatre, looking at the marquee. I said hello and she replied with rather dreamy surprise, "Oh, hello, Professor Halloway." Her hair was dirty and pulled back, revealing a ballerina's chin line. I hadn't realized how thin she was. On her feet she wore those curious black running shoes. She was going into the movie, she said, a Russian film, *Gooseberries*, and although I didn't care particularly for Chekhov, I'd had enough of my own company for one day and I went in with her.

It was crowded in the theatre and we had to sit near the front. During an obnoxious trailer for a summer film I whispered something amusing in her ear, but she appeared not to have heard. Her attention to the screen was absolute. Looking at her upturned face in the flickering light, I was uncomfortably struck with how delicate her features were, a fine sharp nose, full lips, dry and slightly apart. She really *is* lovely, I thought, and I was aware of feeling mildly sad, as if I had lost something.

It was a surprisingly good movie. The actors, I'd heard, had rehearsed it for a number of years on their own initiative. I'd read the story a number of times when I was younger and had been bored by it, but for some reason, perhaps the condition I was in, I responded to it the way you do to a film on an airplane, where you find yourself oddly moved by moments at thirty thousand feet that might make you grimace with condescension back on earth. I was thinking about that when I noticed an odour of perspiration in the air. It was very strong but not at all unpleasant. In fact I found it sort of privately exciting. The notion that I noticed it and she didn't wove a strange veil of intimacy around us.

It was a very warm evening, even in the theatre. She wore a sleeveless summer dress; I was in shirt sleeves, rolled up. Between us stretched a wooden armrest. During a bright outdoor scene I observed with some embarrassment that I had left a glistening sweat stain on the wood. I was in the process of discreetly unrolling my shirt sleeve to wipe it away when Emma, who had been sitting with her hands in her lap, slid her naked forearm over exactly the place where mine had rested. It produced in me the most appalling sensation, a sense of absolute dread. For I was sure she had done it on purpose.

After the film we took a walk through the neighbourhood. We stood in a small alley, talking across the hood of a car, and I noticed a discoloured brick in the wall behind her. I will remember that discoloured brick for the rest of my life, I thought. I walked her home, claiming, I think, that a friend lived in the neighbourhood, that we were planning a symposium on Martin du Gard and that maybe I'd just pop on by and give him a shout. Really, so starchy. And Martin du Gard, no less! But I was terrified, you see. Here I was, a middle-aged professor with a young woman who seemed to admire me. That's what made it so frightening—that I might do something or reveal something that would diminish me in her regard. But she was delightful company, and when we got to her street we stopped for a moment in Sibelius Park and sat on a picnic table. We had talked for a matter of minutes when I suddenly experienced the most overpowering desire to kiss her. My heart positively crashed. I thought what any man would think in my place, that she was going to recoil with horror. Or worse, disappointment. I could almost hear her words in my ears: "Oh, Professor Halloway, you must have misunderstood."

Misunderstood indeed.

But I had already let too many things slip from my fingers, and the notion that I might actually *be* with this young woman, that the only thing standing in my way was the fear that I might put out my hand and have it slapped, the notion that it was perhaps fear alone that stopped me from being happy, was something I knew would haunt me and grind me down for the remainder of my life. So I kissed her. And she kissed me back. And then you know what she said? She said, "Do you want to see my cunt, Professor Halloway?"

She grew up the daughter of an unkempt doctor and his unfaithful wife. From the former she inherited a strange slobbishness, strange because, *à première vue*, she seemed so immaculate, her body anyway, like a Chinese reed, slim, green-eyed, with that mop of straight blonde hair. But if you looked longer you noticed her slightly stooped posture, a button missing from her shirt cuff, her red sweater pulled up at the back; she was a woman who could leave a wet towel on a bed, so to speak. It must have been from her mother (we never got on) that she inherited a sensuality the like of which I'd never really encountered before. Not in so extreme a form anyway. Her lovemaking—and don't worry, I'm not going to embarrass either of us here—was a sort of schizophrenic experience. An authentically *transforming* event. Really, she carried on like a madwoman. She whispered, she swore, she blasphemed, she made demonic requests in a voice that was not her own. "Do you want to see my cunt?" Nice talk, indeed! Imagine taking *that* to the Governing Council dinner. Once, at the opera, she whispered in my ear, "Do you want to know what we used to do at pyjama parties in Ottawa?" *Ottawa* of all places. Our nation's capital! Or that time in the foyer of the chancellor's house—"Do you want to take me from behind?" No, Emma, I don't want to take you from behind, I want to have Christmas pudding with my colleagues. Really, it was unimaginable that it was the same mouth that, only an hour before, had wished her grandmother a happy eighty-seventh birthday. I'll put it this way: sometimes, after going to bed with Emma Carpenter, I wanted to call for an exorcist.

To be honest, it could make her somewhat exhausting, this capacity to be so taken over, this substitution of personalities, as if, in the process of revealing herself, she was exposing to the sunlight an organ so delicate that it seemed still moist from its sheer *internalness*. And while she claimed to have been the one to terminate all her previous romances, I have always harboured the private suspicion that at least some of those men may have been rather relieved to see her go. One couldn't have a comforting little screw with Emma just before one's afternoon nap. No, it was the full spinning head and pea soup, so to speak.

But you quickly became addicted to it. You didn't want her carrying on like that with anyone else. Indeed, she told me a story once that had the curious effect of raising the hair on the back of my neck *for a number of years*. I was quizzing her about old boyfriends, of which there seemed to be a respectable baker's dozen. (She saved the old-girlfriend stories for only the most inappropriate circumstances. To this day I cannot remember a single bar from the third act of *Tosca*, so steamed up was I with prurient speculation.)

But let us return to the boyfriends. Once you start asking about those things, you can't stop; you must have all the details, no matter how scary the whole thing becomes. There was, as I recall, an actor, a lawyer, a football player, a Scottish scientist (here she did a perfect imitation) and so on. And then there was her boss one summer. That's the story that terrified me, as if I were hearing the tale of my own crucifixion. We were walking down a lovely side street in Rosedale. It was a damp day, the leaves smeared on the street. "Have you ever," she began, "made love so much you fainted?"

It was, as my students are fond of saying, a rhetorical question, a sort of trampoline. Sensing trouble, I said no, I hadn't. She gave me a quick sideways glance, and I had the sensation of watching a tail disappear into a hole: if I wanted the beast I would have to grab it now.

And thus it began, a simple enough story from anyone else, but from her slightly dry lips it positively seethed with menace and lechery. "I had just broken up with my boyfriend," she began. "He was a playwright (she named him, a handsome, lush-lipped creature whose face haunted me in theatre lobbies for years after). I liked him, we adored each other's bodies (here I winced), but he was insanely jealous. Just about *everything*. And after a while I couldn't stand it any more. So I broke it off. Anyway, a little while later I moved into his *brother's* house. I don't know why, convenience maybe (ha!). He had a spare room, something like that. Anyway, one Friday afternoon I went out for a drink with my boss after work and we ended up back at my place. At my *new* place. We spent the whole weekend in bed, condoms all over the room, not even getting up to eat. We just fucked all the time." Here I steadied myself on the hood of a car. She looked at me again to see, I think, how the story was taking hold.

"Go on," I croaked.

"When we finally got out of bed and went for something to eat, I fainted on the sidewalk. Just dead away."

For a while I didn't say anything. My stomach was positively churning. I could see Emma getting out of bed, that bony body—it was so extreme, her nakedness, no one ever seemed quite so undressed.

"But, Emma," I said, with escalating heat, "didn't it occur to you that the playwright's brother must have *heard* you making love, must have *told* his brother? Can you imagine? I mean, my Lord, he was jealous to begin with. That must have *killed* him."

It sounded as if I were lecturing her, my voice up an octave and out of breath. But it wasn't moral indignation I was experiencing; it was the realization that I had bitten off perhaps more than I could chew, that here was a woman who could destroy me with no other weapon than my own imagination. I was suddenly aware that a domain of vulnerability existed beneath my feet like a trap door.

"It was over!" she protested.

"How over?"

"I don't know. A couple of weeks. Besides, I was twenty."

*Twenty.*

It was a ridiculous answer, it didn't explain anything; but when you're starving, it's remarkable what will pass for nourishment. I thought about this story for years afterwards, the image of her boss's humping buttocks. Lord! It became a kind of masochistic daydream:

I saw myself, ear to the wall, listening to a hoarse-voiced Emma in the next room saying those *things*. God, how awful!

Anyway, how did I get started on that? I can't remember. But early on, our second or third date, I met her for dinner. It was an upscale restaurant, the second floor of a steak house up near St. Clair Avenue. She ordered a steak, which she left untouched. "I can't eat when I'm around you," she said. "My stomach's too tight." She left a bleeding mouthful at the end of her fork. I knew this was a prelude to something, and after a glass or two of wine she leaned forward and cupped her sharp chin in the palm of her hand. "I have a present for you," she said. I could sense a career-ending opportunity on the horizon and I looked about for witnesses.

She withdrew a ragged T-shirt from her shoulder bag; it had a worn neck and a hole under the arm. "You might need this," she said.

I looked at her and then at it. I must have seemed puzzled. I was. It was obviously a significant gift. But what did it signify?

I sniffed it discreetly. "Ah," I said.

"I just came from the gym."

You see what I mean? An old-fashioned dirty girl, I guess. Or a desk with many drawers, depending on how you see the world. She liked hard-core pornography, read girlie magazines with her hand down her jeans, abused herself on a nightly basis ("I've got it down to a minute. Want to watch?"), lured me into bouts of phone sex, once on a cellphone when I was lunching with a group of visiting professors from Munich. ("Yes, that *does* sound lovely, and we'll chat about it more when I get home.") I don't believe for a second that she was bulimic, but after a half-bottle of wine it gave her a flush of visible pleasure to tell strangers that "For four years I had my finger up my cunt or down my throat." *Vous voyez?*

One evening she borrowed a pullover from me. It was a cool night, the rain had just ceased and I was walking her home. A couple of days later I checked my answering service. After a slightly strangled pause, I heard her say, "I just committed an unnatural act with your sweater."

But it wasn't all good times. She could be, for example, peculiar about her body. About her thinness, which I so adored. Her heart beat at a furious rate; I could hear it sometimes when I had my ear pressed to her chest. It wore her down, I think, the strain of being Emma, and it showed in her hands. She had the hands of an old woman, delicate but colourless. Unhealthy hands. She could lose weight during an afternoon walk down Yonge Street.

One evening, a few months into it, we met at a restaurant for dinner. She was late, which always irritated me, but when she came in the dining room she looked so lovely I forgot my displeasure. I simply couldn't keep my hands off her, nor could I stop talking, and in the course of things I said, "You must order something hearty, anything you want, it's my treat, roast beef, mashed potatoes, something to put some meat on you . . ."

She opened the menu and I remember thinking, Oh, she didn't hear me, I must be talking too much. But then, in a voice I had never heard before, she said, "I'll thank you not to make personal remarks about my body."

*Personal remarks about her body?* Lord, that's all I ever did. My description of her, of how it felt to unbutton her shirt or slip off her socks, had become as graphic as anything she might come out with. I was astonished. And speechless. And embarrassed. There was, in her tone of voice, the implication that she was talking to a cretin.

"Now wait a minute, " I said, in a slightly wobbly voice, but she interrupted me.

"It's not a debate, Darius, it's a matter of manners."

*Manners?*

The evening never recovered, and when she came back to my house she sat deliberately forward on the couch, a most uninviting posture, like a hockey player waiting to be called onto the ice. I put my hand on her back.

"I'm not really comfortable with that tonight," she said. "You've made me feel very self-conscious."

"How could I?" I protested. "I adore you." I leaned over and tried to kiss her ear, but she pulled away with considerable irritation.

"I said no, Darius. All right?"

Oh dear. What a dreadful night. And then she added, "Go into the bedroom and take care of yourself, if you have to. I'll wait out here."

Nice, eh? She was a little touchy, my Emma, sometimes I even thought her a little *touched*, those voices, the foul language, the overheated body, that unpredictable pricklishness. Really, like threading your way through a minefield. But I must say that before her, and I mean all my life before Emma, I had the slightly embarrassing sensation that I was saving myself for someone. I even had it during my marriage. During the actual ceremony I found myself wondering if such-and-such a bridesmaid might be at the reception afterwards. But when I was with Emma, I had the unmistakable feeling that the train had finally pulled into the station. I caught myself being happy.

But we all have a shaming memory, no matter how well we have loved, and I have one too. Emma had gone to the hospital to have her gallbladder out. The day of the operation an article of mine appeared in a prestigious academic journal. I was very excited and rushed to the hospital with it in my hand. She was still groggy from the anaesthetic and was clutching a gold pocket watch. It had belonged to my father. The metal was dull, it no longer kept correct time, but it had a solid, reassuring weight, a beauty from a different era, and I had given it to her the night before for good luck.

The surgeon had done a bad job on her and she raised her nightgown to show an ugly six-inch wound. "Why did they have to cut such a big hole?" she asked, her small blonde head shaking slightly, like an old man's. She waited as if I might know the answer.

But I wasn't paying attention, you see. I wasn't listening. I was thinking about my article and about a rendezvous I was about to have with a colleague, an event where I would be praised. And so I left the hospital. And when I said I was leaving, she went quite still, she appeared to be thinking about something entirely different. Or trying to sort through the anaesthetic to solve a simple mathematics problem. Why didn't she say something? Why didn't she say, No, stay here. I need you?

But she didn't. She swallowed it and in so doing condemned us both.

You don't usually lose someone because of one thing. But that wound, in her stomach and in her heart, never healed. It gave her, I think, a new way of looking at me, that I was *over there*. After that night we were not on the same side any more.

Life went on. We lived together, went on vacation to Thailand. She'd quit graduate school and now worked as a publicist for a small publishing house; I taught my classes. But eighteen months later, perhaps sooner, she walked into the living room late one morning. It was a warm day in winter; there was a high wind, it shook the bare tree branches outside the window, they bobbed up and down in a furious silence, and overhead the clouds whizzed by with unnatural quickness. The mood of the street swung back and forth from gloominess to sprints of sunlight racing down the face of the houses and across the lawns. You couldn't tell if a storm was coming or going.

I was fiddling with a lecture on surrealism, wondering if such and such an anecdote, that business of Alfred Jarry walking a lobster on a leash down the Champs-Elysées, would strike an amusing note for an undergraduate class. "And do you know what Jarry said when asked *why* he was walking a lobster and not a dog?" I waited an anticipatory second. "'Because lobsters don't bark.'"

But Emma appeared not to be listening. This irritated me. She had been moody lately, it came and went without resolution, and the only time I ever heard that gorgeous laugh was when she was on the telephone to a friend.

And I couldn't smell her any more.

"Is there anything wrong?" I asked a bit testily.

Her young eyes watered and she said, "I can't live here any more."

And then I made a very grand mistake, although looking back now, I wonder if it would have mattered. I decided to call her bluff, to be firm but unsympathetic, as if this were a kind of self-indulged aberration, her being so unhappy.

"Then you mustn't," I said.

With theatrical briskness I got up, found my coat and went out to an afternoon movie.

When I came home hours later, the coat hangers in her closet were still clinking, as if there were a wind in the house.

She never reproached me for that scene at the hospital, although something she said a few weeks later still gives me goosebumps. We were in the bedroom, her stitches had just come out, and we were looking silently out the window at a child who was skating around and around on a small ice rink in the park below. The subject of her operation came up and she said, in a voice I barely recognized, "I learned that night that I had a soul. That I had a soul and it lives in my body."

She didn't say anything else or turn her glance away from the skater below. It seemed as if her attention had moved on to something else, that she was trying to solve that mathematical problem again. But I could feel something in my heart contract, and for a second I thought I knew what people mean when they say they can feel someone walking over their grave.

But let me come back to the night she left, the coat hangers still stirring in her cupboard. I had been, as I said, to a movie, and crossing the park toward home (how gloomy it was, the swings rusted and damp) I noticed something in the front window of my house. The Christmas lights! She had left them on and they twinkled merrily in the window, blue, green, red and amber. She had changed her mind! Yes, she had changed her mind and decided to stay after all. I broke into a fast walk, a lump developed in my throat, my eyes watered with things I was going to say. I pulled out my keys. Perhaps I should feign surprise—What! You still here?—but no, not this time. I unlocked the door and burst into the house. Emma! Emma!

But there was no Emma. The Christmas lights flickered over the chesterfield, my desk, the carpet, the notes for my lecture the following day.

Sometime near four in the morning I awoke and the full horror was upon me. I hurried into the bathroom and flicked on the light. In the unnatural brightness I looked like a man escaped from a lunatic asylum. I opened the medicine cabinet and shook a pair of sleeping tablets into my hand, tossed them into my dry mouth. Too impatient to get a glass from the kitchen, I cupped my hands under the cold water tap and sucked noisily. It took two goes.

I phoned her at work the following morning, my voice bounding between hysteria and false bonhomie. I spoke as if somehow this was a shared experience, a ghastly little misunderstanding we were both equally dying to reverse. Comrades in a close call, so to speak.

"So how did *you* sleep last night?" I boomed.

"What do you mean?" she asked simply. Her confusion was authentic, and in it I saw myself bouncing at the end of a rope like a freshly hanged man. If there was a moment when the devil whispered in my ear, "It's over," it was then. It was as if she had gone to sleep and woken up speaking a foreign language, a language I had no access to.

She came over that night. She came over a few times after. I wept. She wept for my weeping. And then she went home. She called it that, home, this bed in a friend's apartment. She left our place and she went home.

Morning after morning I woke up too early, the snow blowing sideways, the day stretching ahead of me. Stretching and stretching and stretching all the way to the horizon where, if you looked, you could make out a tiny, crooked tree. I taught my classes. I stared into the fireplace and waited for the phone to ring. Days went by, then weeks. Hollowed out by worry and a kind of relentless anxiousness that cut through everything, I lost weight. My pants hung from my hips. I stabbed a new hole in my belt buckle.

One night, unable to last another second, I snatched up the phone and called her. "Where *are* you?" I cried. She hurried over; I proposed marriage; she diplomatically declined; offered sex instead, which I gratefully embraced. But she was so *silent*! Looking at her young body in the bed, I swear the notion of losing her forever made me feel as if I might go mad. And then she went home.

For a while, as long as I could smell her on my hands, I felt better. But then it all started up again. I could feel the panic seize me around the ribs, slowly, like a snake, and I could hear that dreadful whisper in my ear, "She's gone," the last syllable like a poof when a candle is extinguished. She's gone.

I listened to opera. I listened to Bach. On Wednesdays I went to a Cajun bar; the music excited me. I'd have one, two, three mugs of beer, the accordion shrieked, the band reeled, and I could feel my shoulders coming down. The room softened; the lights glowed; I could breathe. Yes, she'd come back. She'd be back. Just be patient. Ah yes, be patient with her. But when I came outside, the winter bared its teeth at me; the wind slapped my face; giant icicles loomed like tusks overhead; and by the time I arrived home I was frightened and sober. And there was never, never, never a message from her.

Spring came, and one fragrant afternoon I sat in the park watching a child whisper to a cat and waited for Emma to come. I sat on a picnic table, the same picnic table I had kissed her on four years before, and watched her pedal toward me on her bicycle.

Upstairs in my house (God, she was beautiful), I leaned forward in my chair, she on the couch, my fingers steepled beneath my chin, and began a practised speech. I said that she had been gone for some three months now, and three months for someone who is waiting is a long time. She nodded in silent agreement. I went on to say that when we did see each other, it was always at my behest, as it had been again that day. More nodding. She too was prepared, you could see that. She'd been on the phone (that mother again) and from the way she listened, the measured patience, I had the feeling she had reached a final decision, had perhaps a long time ago but had only now consented to the language to describe it accordingly. I wound up by saying that I didn't need kid gloves or kind treatment but simply the truth. I opened my mouth to say more, but nothing came out, which was good because there wasn't any more to say.

She took a moment, looked at the floor to assemble her thoughts, and said, "I am leaning in the direction of not being in love with you any more."

To this day I'm not sure I've ever heard of such a bizarre notice of termination, ever. *Leaning in the direction of not being in love with you any more*. But I had spent too many sweaty nights, smoked too many cigarettes, lost too many pounds to allow for any ambiguity. And so I said, slowly and deliberately, looking at her pale and beautiful face, "Does that mean you *don't* love me any more?"

"Yes," she said crisply. She *was* prepared.

"Does that mean you don't want me any more?"

"Yes," she said again.

"These are terrible words, Emma."

"Yes."

"Is there anyone else?" I asked. "Or did I lose you all on my own?"

"All on your own," she said with a smile.

She offered me a sexual favour, which I accepted, but I had just begun a new medical prescription and I could not see it to completion. She stayed a while longer, although I can't imagine what we talked about.

"I shan't walk you downstairs," I said as she hovered in the bedroom doorway. Those were my last words to her. I lay in bed, looking down on the park, and I heard the front door close and then creak open. She came back and pulled it to firmly. I fancied, a few moments later, that I heard the rattle of her bicycle chain as she unlocked it and pulled it through her spokes, circling her saddle with it and locking it again. Yes, the window was open, I must have heard it. Then absolute silence, a parking lot reaching all the way to the horizon.

CHAPTER 4

For the first few days I wandered about in a state of relief. At least I *knew*. But then it started up again, waking in the morning too early, imagining her in bed with her boss, spread-eagled in ecstatic, name-calling abandon. I knew enough about bodies and their predictability to know that no matter how much a woman adores you, she will invariably end up repeating her favourite repertoire in the bed of the man who replaces you. A thought that, when it struck, made me want to sit down in the street.

I went to the doctor and got a dose of stronger sleeping pills. My appetite was gone and I continued to lose weight. Students began to comment on it. I told them I had taken up jogging. I began to worry that lack of sleep and weakness were going to cost me my job. At a spring book sale a chap from the Department of Semiotics took a photograph of me and pinned it up in the faculty lounge. With uncharacteristically high cheekbones and sunken eyes, my horror dwelt in plain sight.

Women were strangely drawn to me. On the subway one evening I noticed a dark-haired woman staring at me. Normally I'm very shy, but I struck up a conversation with her. It didn't matter what she thought of me. When we arrived at my platform, I invited her with breathtaking nonchalance to take a coffee with me. Of course she accepted. We talked for an hour, she came back to my house and we went to bed. It went quite well. Aha, I thought, this is how to do it: cure a sexual wound sexually. But when I saw her a second time a few days later, I didn't like her face when she laughed, her prominent pink gums. I wondered how I'd missed them in the first place.

Soon afterwards a high school teacher solicited my attention in the corner grocery store. I'd seen her many times before, a narrow-shouldered woman with skin so pale it was almost blue. Living with Emma, I'd often watched her wander up the street after school, always dressed in black, and I'd entertained some rather guilty day-dreams about her. There was a particular thing I wanted to do to her. *En tout cas*, I took her to dinner at an Italian restaurant on Baldwin Street. We had a bottle of wine, then another. I drank most of it. It went splendidly, and near eleven, the wine glowing on my face, she drove me back to my house and parked her car in the driveway. We came in the side door, and something about the way I moved, the series of habitual movements from sticking my key in the doorknob and turning it simultaneously to pushing open the door, which made a very particular squeak, to clicking on the hall light with my right hand, the keys making the same jingle they always made, suggested to me, to my body, rather, that I was coming home with Emma after another night at our local restaurant. And suddenly the notion that I was taking *another* woman through this sacred ritual struck me as obscene and indecent. But I was too frightened to be left alone with my own thoughts, so I offered her a drink and we settled in the living room, on the same couch where Emma had read *Anna Karenina*. But when I kissed her, the high school teacher, when she leaned forward and closed her eyes in a manner I thought a trifle theatrical, she smelt funny. I don't mean bad. I just mean odd. Different. The French get most things wrong, but they're right about love: it really *is* a question of smell. And when I did that thing to her that I had day-dreamed about doing, I was shocked at how extraordinarily different women's bodies are, one from another.

She left shortly after that, but we stayed friends. We even had a drink together every so often until she got a boyfriend, and then things dried up and blew away the way they do.

It was the strangest thing, though; it was as if women could see the pain on my face and were drawn to it. I think they felt safe with me. Whereas men, men I avoided. They meant well, but in showing me they understood, they said terrible things. I know they were try-ing to lighten things up, but they did more harm. Once, at the end of an evening of cards, the host walked me to the door and, just as I was about to set off up the street, stopped me.

"How are things with Emma?" he asked.

I spluttered, I made light of it. I felt myself growing smaller and tighter with each sentence. Picking up on my mood, my host scrutinized my features with wide-eyed delight.

"One *does* move on," I said finally, with a certain successful elegance, but even as the words issued from my mouth, I saw the image of her boss's quivering bottom, complete, of course, with Emma's ghastly "you're-just-a-bad-boy-with-a-big-hard-cock" soundtrack.

I walked home double time, as if the motion of my body might stop the images from coming into too clear a focus.

It seemed as if I were radiating some peculiar kind of pollen. I went to New York to see an opera and came home with the stewardess from the airplane. Never in my life had I had such extraordinary luck with women. I can't remember her name, I never saw her again, but when she left my bed, I lay in the dark in the unfamiliar smell of her perfume and felt a shiver of excitement, like a prisoner granted a new trial.

I slept like a dreamless dead weight that night, and in the morning I was famished. I hurried down the street and took breakfast in a new restaurant. I chatted happily to the owner, offered insights into the neighbourhood. In the middle of a sentence I looked out the window and saw a bicycle locked to a fire hydrant and thought to myself, Look, look at this, I'm looking at a bicycle locked to a hydrant, I'm not thinking about *that other thing* at all.

They were so kind to me, those women. How I would miss them later when the horror was gone from my face and they no longer *saw* me.

There were oddballs too, a hippie girl who followed me home from a lawn sale and after only the barest preliminaries asked me to spank her.

"How *old* are you?" I asked.

"Twenty-eight," she said.

"Don't you think this is, well, a little *much* for a first date?" She looked baffled. I went on. "Perhaps this is more like fifth- or sixth-date stuff."

"All my friends do it," she said.

"Is this a sort of generational thing?"

Her laughter spilt richly into the air. "How do you mean?"

"It's a damn curious thing, that's all. When I was your age . . ." But I stopped there. Just those words, this groaning overture, drained me, and I could feel myself fading, right in front of her eyes, like an old sign on an inn.

"That must have been some time ago," she said. "No offence."

I took none and obliged her, securing her feet to the bedpost with a Cambridge necktie, the rationale being that I might find in this unfamiliar landscape a distraction from Emma, the sensation of whose absence had returned like a toothache. Even as I lowered the young lady's panties, even as I raised my hand to her backside, I was aware of Emma's heart beating somewhere in the city. A parallel existence to mine.

When my little hippie left the house, massaging her smouldering pink fanny, she gave her hair a toss like a pony and asked if I'd buy a dog collar and a doormat for next time. "I have a fantasy," she

37

began, standing in the doorway. "I want to lie by your front door just like a big dog, an Afghan maybe, and wait for you to come home."

"Really?" I said. This was astonishing, and for a second it really *did* stop me from thinking about Emma.

"When I hear something at the door," she went on (it was all quite worked out), "I'll jump up, like this"—now raising her hands to her chest and flopping them over like paws—"and if it's just the mailman, I'll be so disappointed! I'll just have to go back to my mat and lie down and wait some more."

I looked at her carefully. She didn't seem insane. In fact, in her yellow summer dress, she was quite pretty, with a long face and freckles on her cheekbones. Perhaps it *was* a generational thing. Perhaps this was how young people got to know each other these days.

"I think you're out of my league," I said softly, and touched her gently on the elbow.

"Oh," she said. "Goodbye then," and she offered me her cheek to kiss.

A year later, when the spell had worn off and women were no longer drawn to me, I tracked her down in a small Ontario town and phoned her. Knowing ahead of time what the answer would be, still I asked her, a tad too gingerly, if she was planning on coming back to Toronto. No, she wasn't. She was getting married. A local boy, no less, a pharmacist.

But that was still a long way off.

In the midst of all this a strange thing happened. Serrault knocked on my office door one afternoon and came in. He was wearing a dark shirt with a black knit tie, chic but not ostentatious, and I thought to myself, ah, he pays more attention to his clothes than I assumed. In a rather serious tone of voice—you could see he was uncomfortable—Serrault said, "Ah, look, Darius . . . Emma has phoned, and she wanted me to tell you to be sure to change the air filter on the stove."

"What?" I said.

He waited a moment before answering. "Apparently there is some risk of fire if you don't change it every year or so."

"The air filter on *my* stove? *À moi?*"

"Yes."

"But that's rather bizarre that she would call you about a thing like that."

He shrugged tactfully. He was going to add something, a pleasantry I'll bet, but thought better of it.

"Am I supposed to phone her back or anything?"

"She didn't say, specifically. But perhaps yes, for clarification." Here a smile. "You know where the filter is?" he went on. He tilted his hands into a box as if to show me. "Right above the grill, there is a—"

*"Non, je sais, je sais."*

"Well then . . ."

"Still, it's very mysterious."

He did that thing that Frenchmen do with their mouths, and shrugged. Sensing his presence might provoke still more questions (for which he knew there could be no satisfactory response), he withdrew.

For a few days I waited with considerable urgency. I was convinced this business with the air filter signalled something important, a shift, a rope thrown between two ships. Perhaps it meant that Emma missed me so profoundly that she was seeking an excuse, no matter how indirect, to contact me. I thought of phoning her. Who knows? Maybe the danger was real. Maybe the thing might actually *catch on fire*!

But it didn't. It never did anything. I didn't get around to replacing the air filter for years, five or six at least, and nothing ever happened. Nothing whatsoever.

A month went by. It was August. I wrote a paper on the irony of genius—I had Céline in mind—which was accepted by the *Harvard Quarterly*. But this time out it offered me only the most momentary distraction. I had forgotten about it by dinner of the same day.

Coming home one summer night, I opened my mailbox at the side of the house. By now I was waiting for a letter from Emma. It was maddening, but I knew I'd never be free of her, that I'd keep on waiting, stupidly, pointlessly, until I knew she'd slept with someone else. I was sure she knew that. When it happened, she'd tell me. But there was nothing there, and in a cloud of self-pity I kicked open the side door of my house. "I have a *shit* life," I said to anyone who was listening.

To comfort myself I rented the video of *Gooseberries*, the first movie I'd seen with Emma. When I got to the part where I remembered her slipping her forearm over the damp armrest, I stopped the movie and retreated to my bedroom, from which I emerged moments later clear-headed and hungry. I dreamt about her *all night* and in the morning sadness sat on my chest. I could hardly drag myself from bed. I took the movie back to the store and dropped it in the overnight box like an out-of-date passport.

Around this time, after loathing him for years—a sissy and a momma's boy—I found myself fascinated by Marcel Proust. I reread *Un amour de Swann* as if I were reading my own gravestone, obsessed to know, for I had long forgotten, if he got the girl in the end. For his fate would be mine, I was sure of it.

Some nights, sweating, my calf twitching as if tiny aliens were moving about under the skin (for a while I believed it happened when Emma was making love to someone, that the nerves in my leg were like some invisible antennae that picked from the very air the vibrations of her betraying me ten blocks away), I'd find myself sinking down into sleep. But when I'd almost arrived, was almost beyond all reach, I experienced a kind of physical halting, as if I had landed on a subterranean roof or, more precisely, had come to the end of a thick elastic band that pulled me suddenly upwards, a small, almost punitive bounce, as if to say, no, you shall think about Emma some more.

I recalled somewhat bitterly that the February she left me, I had fussed about all sorts of things. Being passed over for the keynote speech at a Lisbon symposium. A crack that Serrault made, impugning, I thought, my affection for the poetry of Jacques Prévert.

*Ce genre de connerie.* All nonsensical pricks and stabs. How odd that of all the catastrophes I nursed, it was that one alone that never occurred to me. Like a train, I suppose, the sound appearing to come from the *other* direction. Suddenly there it is, black and seven storeys high and upon you.

Lord, it was hot that summer, rivulets of perspiration running down my chest, morning and night, my face puffy from the heat. Tree branches flopped over like bad hair. From my porch I watched my neighbour's yellow cat batting the lower bushes for moths. One motionless evening I caught a whiff of myself running up the stairs from the laundry room. I was starting to *smell* like Emma.

I went to a psychiatrist, a former Princeton professor, something of an addiction expert, *on disait.* But he chain-smoked, and when I commented on it, he informed me briskly that there were plenty of psychiatrists in the city who didn't smoke. His appearance was strange enough, the long jaw, that dank hair so peculiar to English intellectuals, but his voice, my Lord, high-pitched, like air escaping from a baboon's anus. How such a creature had been called, much less encouraged, into the business of mental health eluded me. But not everyone apparently. Serrault had recommended him. Thought he was *un type intéressant.*

"You're a man whose exquisite pet has run away," said the doctor in his strange whale voice.

"But I loved her!" I insisted.

"People love their pets," he said.

An exquisite pet? Emma? My Emma.

I listened; I disputed. Terrors spewed from my mouth like pus from a lanced boil.

"Look at the state you've got yourself into," he declared, and gave me a pill to put under my tongue. When I left his office, it was with a handshake and a light step that carried me to the elevator and down nine floors and out onto the street where dusk gathered in the corners of red brick buildings. It was remarkable. I could feel my appetite return. I called a friend to meet me for dinner. I picked a restaurant Emma and I had often gone to. I felt invulnerable, as if somehow, by talking so candidly, I had flushed the poison from my system. I showered. I dressed in a snappy blue shirt and dark slacks. Rooting through my cupboard for a pair of fancy shoes, something to gild the occasion, I suddenly remembered the pill I'd taken in the doctor's office. Surely *not*. I phoned his office, but he had gone for the day. I phoned a pharmacy and asked how long such and such a drug would last, its effects. An hour at most, they said. I looked at my watch. Look—it was almost two hours. I must be free of it. Cured!

I went for dinner. I talked merrily. The city, the streets were mine again. It lasted until bedtime. Then, like a fast-growing rust, the kind you might see on speeded-up film, the nervous jangle came back. I took another pill. I put it under my tongue and lay motionless in the dark, and it was as if a black beast was slowly backing out of my bedroom, the snorts and the scratch of claws on the wooden floor growing fainter and fainter.

Three days later, having burned through an entire month's prescription, I returned to the baby-voiced doctor for an encore. We tried something else, I forget its name, but it made me perspire like a madman at night. I woke up two, three times to find my T-shirt soaked, the sheet under me dark with sweat. For a while I wondered if I'd contracted AIDS. For a while, and this is shameful to say, I sort of hoped I had.

We tried Valium, then Lectopam, then a green tablet that left a bitter taste in my mouth as it came on. I used to look forward to that taste. I'd take the tablet in a café at the foot of my street. I'd nurse a beer and a cigarette and then that funny taste came on and I'd pay up and hurry home through the warm air and get into bed before it wore off. But I'd wake up an hour and a half later. My terror, my loneliness, the haunting *absoluteness* with which Emma had vanished from my life (sometimes she was so near I felt like I could open up my eyes and she'd be there, breezy and sunny, come back from the store or the library; she was so near I could almost touch her) cut clean through the drug.

They came at me very hard, those moments; they clutched my heart till I had no breath in my body. Once I took a graduate class to the film of Émile Zola's *Germinal*. Movies are not for the heartbroken, I had forgotten that. The eyes rest on the vivid images, but instead of being absorbed by them, they use the screen as a sort of trampoline for private, painful imaginings. The stillness in the theatre, the privacy that comes from being in the dark give rise to a focused torture. I imagined myself floating like a disembodied soul through Emma's new apartment. It was just before dawn. I glided over her black running shoes inside the front door, her daybook on the front hall table with that small handwriting. I moved through the kitchen with its stubby fridge, pictures of her and her friends stuck to the door with magnets. No picture of me. I hesitated at the bedroom door, heard the swish of a limb rubbing against a sheet. I went in, passing between the wooden molecules until I was on the other side. Grey daylight covered her hairbrush, her watch, her rings on a chair beside the bed. Why would she remove her rings? I peered through the darkness. She lay on her back, her arm crooked over her head, her knees up, supporting the sheet like a tent. During the night the sheet had fallen to her waist. It must have been a warm night, even for summer. But why had she removed her rings? Suddenly, involuntarily, I saw her hand, those delicate fingers wrapped around something obscene, pumping it slowly up and down while she sought her boss's eyes. *Do you want to see my cunt?*

Rising from my seat as if I'd been violently pinched from below, I hurried down the row, stepping over legs, *sorry, so sorry*, and rushed up the centre aisle. Bursting into the lobby, I took the escalator downstairs, ran along the hall to a kiosk and bought a package of cigarettes. I sat down at the back of a café. I opened the pack with trembling fingers. I struck the match once, twice, three times. But my fingers were too damp. I pulled another match loose. It lit, I puffed, the tobacco caught. I inhaled a deep lungful. But then, as if I'd just heard an unexpected noise, like a deer alerted in the forest, I had the alarming certainty that I was moments, seconds from an encounter with Emma's friends. I imagined a group of them walking quickly through the mall; they'd be on their way to a summer camp reunion, or buying a present for a friend's wedding, and they'd notice—it'd only take one of them—they'd notice me puffing like a madman in the Café Sweet Time. Of course, they'd stop to speak to me. They were like that. Polite with the overcheerfulness of former students. They'd come over, the whole bloody bunch of them. Alison and Robin and Susan and Trish and Emily Jane. Emily Jane? What kind of fucking name is that? The missing Austen sister? They'd tell Emma they saw me smoking cigarettes. He doesn't smoke, does he? No, I didn't think so. Mystified, knowing glances. He must be a mess, poor man. And Emma, shaking her head with concern, no, no, that's true, he doesn't smoke. Mind you, I haven't seen him for ages.

*I am leaning in the direction of not being in love with you any more.*

I left the café and went around the corner to a bank of pay telephones. And there, hunched over the last phone, my back to the world, a phone line humming expectantly in my ear, I puffed and puffed and puffed.

CHAPTER 5

Someone moved into the house next door. He had two dogs, terriers or something, and in the morning when he went to work, he left them in the backyard. All day long they went *yip, yip, yip*. I was in my study preparing for a graduate seminar on Symbolism and Impressionism (the course had been dropped on me at the last moment) when it began to irk me. One never knows why, at a certain moment, neither the one before nor the one after, the nervous system suddenly, like an eel peeping forth from his crevice, takes note of an intruder.

Taking a different tack this time, a concession, no doubt, to my evolving sense of community, I slipped a note in the letter box mentioning, very politely, the racket and how, after a couple of hours, it "got on the nerves." I didn't leave my name or a phone number, but I was, as I said, *énormément poli*. I got a peek at the dogs, too. They were small, hairy beasts tied to a long leash. None too bright either. They stood in the middle of the yard, looking at the back door and barking, as if their master might emerge at any second and let them in.

After my note I waited a couple of days. Nothing happened. *Yip, yip, yip.*

So I wrote another letter, this time on a colleague's computer. I used an unusual typeface not found on my system. I said, in no uncertain terms, that his dogs were becoming a bother, that if he didn't find some way to "clam them up," I was going to call the Society for the Prevention of Cruelty to Animals. I considered the expression "clam them up" a prudent choice. In the event of something untoward happening, no one would give me a second look. After all, why would a man of my stature use a cretin's turn of phrase?

I dropped the note in his box, this time after dark. I didn't want the neighbours spotting me. I live in a Portuguese neighbourhood and those women, once their husbands die, do nothing but snoop at the window.

I heard barking the next morning. I woke up instantly, as if my body had been waiting, like an animal in the dark. It wasn't even six, I could tell by the light. There's a lonely clarity to sunlight when it's too early. He—I assumed it was a he—must have let the hounds out early, a kind of middle finger to whoever wrote the note. I went to the other end of my house and got into the bed in the guest room. I like the way the sheets smell in there; it's comforting, like a hotel. Still, I didn't get to sleep until I figured a course of action. Then I went under as if dropped overboard with an anchor around my ankles.

I didn't want to go to a hardware store in my neighbourhood, so I took the streetcar to Parkdale. I had a flat out there years ago, but my memory isn't what it used to be and I got off at the wrong stop. Everything seemed moved around. Finally I found the place (next door to where that red-haired girl worked in the donut shop—what a foolish business that was) and waited in the paint section for the attendant to free himself. He was an effeminate black man, very good at his job and he knew it. I explained I had a rat in my basement; I wanted to dispatch him, painlessly if possible.

"Shoot him," the man said, "only watch out for the ricochet."

I had the impression he had said this before and I allowed myself a small riposte. "We don't want to kill *all* the rats down there after all."

"Right," he said, and laughed the way people do when they don't follow you. Or don't think you're funny perhaps, although in this case I'm confident it was the former. He knew precisely what I wanted and where it was in the store, as I suspect he knew the whereabouts of everything. He led me to a shelf of small, chocolate-bar-sized packages in different colours, for ascending lethalness, I assumed. I bought the yellow pack, went to a butcher's on Roncesvalles and bought a pound of fatty hamburger—fat makes the hamburger more flavourful—and came home, picking up some tenderizer at the corner.

After putting my purchases on the kitchen counter, I locked the door and lowered the living-room blinds. I unwrapped the bar. It was a colourless wafer, very hard. I tried to snap it in half but couldn't. My face reddened; the effort left white indentations in my fingers. Finally

I sawed it in two with a serrated paring knife and grated it into a fine yellow powder. I scrubbed the grater myself afterwards in soapy hot water and rinsed it thoroughly. The notion of accidentally killing myself with a poisoned omelette made me smile. I wished I had someone to share the joke with. I thought of one of my students, Edmond, his plump legs lounged over the edge of a chair, high on God knows what, tapping his prominent Adam's apple. Only the other day he asked me why I didn't just quit, go off somewhere and write poetry. Really, sometimes I have a mind to throw him out of my office and tell him to come back in four years when he's not so bloody naïve. But I think I'd rather miss him. Besides, he's quite right: *Thérèse Raquin* is bullshit.

Anyway, while drying the grater and hanging it back on its proper hook, I felt a kind of energized purpose, and I realized it had been some time since I'd felt it.

Near five that afternoon I cooked up a pair of patties, rare, *saignant* even, but perhaps a little overspiced, and put them in a plastic bag. I pulled my car in front of my house and made a great production of "preparing to leave for the weekend." I left the car doors open, Rachmaninov thundering on the radio while I trundled out a small suitcase and a half-dozen thick books, which I laid carefully in the back seat. A working weekend.

My neighbour from across the street drifted out onto his patio and joined me on the sidewalk. He's a lawyer now, but until recently he was a local politician, some say a bagman for the incumbent party, but I know nothing of these matters and besides, I couldn't care less.

In his socks and sandals and blue shorts he looked like a high school teacher. We exchanged pleasantries, but he kept throwing little glances at my new neighbour's house, and finally he asked me what I made of it. I asked, of what? "Those fucking dogs," he replied.

This was good, but it was also important to play it right. I paused theatrically and then, as if I had just caught a faint sound, a sound as remote as electricity passing through the wires overhead, I said agreeably, "Oh yes, you're right."

Right about what? It was intended to flatter, but he looked mildly irritated with me. "Come *on*," he said, pleasantly unpleasant. "You must have heard them." He sounded rather peevish and for a second I thought I saw what the voters had seen when they tossed him out of office.

"I'm sure they're just getting used to the neighbourhood," I said.

This expression of exasperating—and idiot—goodwill struck entirely the right note. It was succinct and easy to remember. When I turned the corner at the foot of my street, I caught a glimpse of my neighbour, his arms crossed, glaring at the house next door.

I drove north. It being a Friday, the traffic was heavy until I cleared the city and then a sad, golden light spread over the farmhouses and the gorgeous fields. The air smelt clean and young, and I remembered taking Emma out to these fields once just after we'd met and snuggling in a sleeping bag under the bright sky. "I don't give a shit about Verlaine," she said. "I just want to pump your cock till you faint." Quite the nature girl, my Emma. But it was so lovely out there. Particularly after the fireworks, after Satan had withdrawn and she'd become human again. You could smell the damp earth that night and the air and Emma's saliva-wet face; you could hear the night sounds of a farmer's field. It was so *raw*, it seemed as if a finger passed through your chest and touched you in some humming place.

It was after dark when I heard the stones crackle under the wheels of my car as I left the highway and followed a gravel lane for a quarter of a mile, a slow, curving route, the trees rising on each side, hundreds and hundreds of little circular leaves glimmering like coins in the headlights. After gliding to a stop in a dark parking lot, I turned off the car lights and the radio and found myself thinking, quite incongruously, of a waitress who had served me years ago on an outdoor patio. She had the oddest name, Constance something. Someone had phoned, I gathered, a customer, claiming to have left behind a handbag under my table, and she had come over and while searching the floor had rested her hand very gently on my shoulder to keep her balance. There was something about her touch, a combination of absolute lightness and at the same time familiarity, as if she had touched me many times, knew me well, was very comfortable doing it. I flushed with pleasure and desire, like a cat stroked by his master. Moreover, I had the sensation that only someone who loved me could touch me like that. Constance *Guitar*, that was her name. I'm sure she never gave me another thought, not from the moment she turned her back on my table, but now, out in the parking lot, I experienced a ghostly longing for her. The hotel rose up before me, floodlit and purring with people, and I caught myself daydreaming that she was with me, that the two of us were coming here for the weekend together. How happy that would be. What fun. With her turned-around baseball cap and that curiously theatrical voice, she'd have enjoyed this place.

I checked in and took a table for dinner, which overlooked a fast-running river and, downstream, an abandoned mill, whose facade was illuminated like a movie set by a bank of lights. From where I sat, you could hear the water sluicing over the dam. I treated myself to an overpriced Pinot Noir, Oak Knoll '92, and just the expectation of its arrival cheered me up. After a glass and a bit the fireflies came out. The candle flames wavered like caramel. The dining room seemed warmer, the people pleasant and animated.

Near eleven I repaired to my room. I was a little wobbly from the wine and a heated cognac, and for a while I sat on my bed, looking, I'm afraid, like Jack Nicholson near the end of *The Shining*. But in truth I was trying to explain to myself, to track down the reasons for that bout of sadness that had struck me so poignantly in the parking lot. And after a while I recalled an event that had happened near the beginning of my career. I had gone to Budapest to give a lecture on the fraudulent French poet Lautréamont, an authentic no-talent who, for some bewildering reason, had come into fashion in the sixties. (Of that suicidal bunch only Arthur Rimbaud was the real item.) It was a very prestigious invitation, or so I had persuaded myself at the time. (In the world of academia, when you describe your colleagues as brilliant and an occasion as prestigious, you are inevitably talking about yourself and where you belong.) *De toute façon*, an hour before I was scheduled to take the podium, I found myself wandering in the old quarter of the city. Everything was decaying, parapets, churches; the narrow lanes mouldy and wet. I saw a child pulling a wagon over the cobblestones, his face a dark, unsmiling tulip, and suddenly I was steeped in sadness. Memories from my childhood illuminated themselves like small films: a flag drooping on a schoolyard pole, a girl in a square dress running across the kindergarten playground, a fat man oiling my tricycle. Other memories crowded in.

I walked and walked and saw nothing of old Budapest. What is wrong with me, I wondered, why am I so *sad*? Finally, staring sightlessly into the window of a second-hand bookstore, I realized what it was: I was *scared*. Scared that my lecture might fall on unsympathetic ears, that my audience might find in it confirmation of what I already knew, that I was second-rate.

Sitting motionless in my hotel room thirty-odd years later, the river running by the old mill, I realized I had fallen into that familiar pond again. I was frightened.

Still, it was time to go.

I roused myself and went down the back stairs, out the side door, and circled the magnificent hotel, avoiding its floodlights until I found my car. I drove back to the city in silence.

I parked ten blocks from my house. No one was about. It was a humid night, the air, especially after the country, clammy and dead. I cut through a back lane of rundown garages and unlocked a wooden door that led into my backyard, crossed the damp grass quickly and sought cover in the lilac bushes near my kitchen window.

I opened the plastic grocery bag. I could smell the tenderizer. I eased my hand in and removed a baseball-sized patty.

A light went on in an upstairs window. I withdrew deeper into the bushes. A woman looked out over the yard. From the desk lamp beneath her you could see she had red, almost electrified hair. I hadn't expected a woman. She was talking to someone in the room, smiling and looking over her shoulder. Then the other person stepped into the frame. With blonde hair and a sharp nose she reminded me of Emma, the way she held herself, the slightly rounded shoulders, the head jutted a bit forward. The desk lamp went out; the backyard fell back into darkness.

I waited five minutes, maybe longer, then lobbed the patty into the yard. Then a second one. I returned quickly to the car, wiping my hands on a rag in the trunk. I should have worn gloves. All the way back I could smell the hamburger on my hands. I couldn't help sniffing my fingers to see if it was still there.

Back in my hotel room it was three in the morning. A bird chirped nearby. I poured myself a cognac from the mini-bar, opened the windows, lay on the bedspread and stared out at the starry night, my glass on my chest. The river raced downstream. At daylight I could still smell my hands.

CHAPTER 6

I've always thought I was going to die in a plane crash, but a kind of beguiling calm overtook me this time as the wheels lifted from the tarmac and we arced sickeningly upwards. I saw my life as something falling away from me like the earth below and I thought, yes, maybe now's *not* such a bad time to go. I looked around the cabin and wondered if people about to die in a plane crash look different from regular passengers. I looked for a pallor, a horror, an animalism. But it wasn't there. It was a cheerful crowd, secretaries and their rat-tailed boyfriends all tired, all mildly anxious, just like me.

I ordered a Bloody Mary. I dumped in the whole ounce of vodka, gave it a stir and took a sip. It was strong and made me shudder with disgust. But I persevered, and by midway through the drink I felt something loosen in my shoulders, something kick free in my head, as if a rope had been cut and the boat had drifted out into the

stream. But travel is a terrible aphrodisiac, all that worry, the bouncing about, whatever, and before too long I caught sight of a skinny,
flat-chested young woman sitting on the aisle a row up from me.
I don't quite know how to put this intelligently, but there was a kind
of chipmunk cuteness about her that quite hypnotized me. She was
travelling with her husband and she half slumbered on his shoulder
while he read a magazine. He looked like a pleasant chap, really, with
a small, handsome head and bright eyes. He turned around at one
point and I dropped my glance so violently I startled the woman
next to me.

But I couldn't keep my eyes off her, as if, by staring long enough
and hard enough, I could somehow neutralize her terrible power. I
imagined the most graphic images of her body. I wanted to devour
her naked feet. By the time the plane landed, my hands were shaking and I felt such a sense of urgency, panic even, that I broke the
line and stepped over the rope barrier to buy a package of cigarettes
in the airport bar. After a few puffs I could feel myself grow calmer,
dreamier, as the tobacco stole into my blood. I took a deep breath
and looked around. I couldn't see her anywhere. I felt a dull stirring of
relief, as if I had just gotten out of trouble or solved a problem.

I cleared Customs and walked across the tarmac to the bus, the
jungle screaming green, the birds screeching, everything hollering
*hurry up, hurry up*. It took a couple of hours to get to the hotel, but
it seemed interminable, a life chapter almost, the scorching highway,
the compulsory rainfall (how depressing the tropics are under a
cloudy sky), the exquisite sunset and so on. I hurried to the front of

the check-in line, stepping over golf bags and expensive suitcases. I may even have elbowed a grandmother out of the way, but I wanted to get to my room, and quickly. That's the great illusion of travel, of course, the notion that there's somewhere to *get to*. A place where you can finally say, Ah, I've arrived. (Of course there is no such place. There's only a succession of waitings until you go home.)

I threw my bag and my feather pillow (I always travel with my own pillow, it tricks my body into thinking I'm at home) onto the bed, turned on the air conditioner, ignored the damp smell in the room and hurried down to the bar.

It was an outdoor patio. Cicadas shrieked in the moist foliage, tourists moved in worried clumps. The heat was terrible. I pried myself between two red-faced Brits. I ordered a beer and tried to light a cigarette, but my fingers gummed up the paper and it shredded. I lit another. I took an enormous drag, smoke funnelled into my lungs and a kind of nausea filled my whole being. Everything went flat and grey. Turning my back to the crowd, I stepped away from the bar and retched. My eyes watered. I stepped discreetly behind a tree and threw up in the bushes. Welcome to the Caribbean.

I went back to my room, thought perhaps I'd wait until the nicotine lifted and then give the evening another shot. But I didn't like the way my room smelt; it was musty or something. I sneezed, then sneezed again. I looked at myself in the mirror. My face was bright red. I opened the doors and turned off the light and got into bed and tried to sleep. I imagined a particularly intimate act with the flat-chested girl on the plane. That often does the trick, but I was too itchy, especially the soles of my feet. I scratched one foot with the other, to no avail. It was as if there were sand fleas under the sheet. Or ticks maybe. I got up and shut the window. Perhaps they were coming in off the beach. I got back into bed. For a second my feet stopped itching and I lay in peace, but then there was a bang right below me and the sound of grinding metal. I opened the French doors and looked down. On the floor below me, the second floor, I saw a light spread out on the sand. The clanking and banging continued. It was an air conditioner, a faulty air conditioner. It clanked and rattled all night. I could get hardly any sleep.

In the morning I complained to the concierge. He offered to move me but couldn't; there were no spare rooms, only villas at the far end of the property. But they were two hundred U.S. a night. I went down to the pool and read and stared about and saw, to my horror, the girl from the plane walk across the hot patio and sit in a lounge chair right in front of me. Her husband followed soon after. I moved my chair to face the ocean, but I couldn't stop looking at her. She wore a sleeveless white T-shirt, and I knew that in a second she was going to do something that would make me feel quite ill. And it did.

Settling in her chair, pointing it this way and then that, she put her hands behind her head and closed her eyes. But then, with a sudden gesture, as if startled, she sat up and ripped off her T-shirt. It was one of those awful places where women don't wear tops. Christ, the stress of it! My pale, skinny friend sat forward in her deck chair and began to cover herself, her small breasts, under her arms, her neck, her thighs with suntan lotion while her husband flipped through what appeared to be a copy of *The Economist*. Really, I thought, if he were half a man he would take her upstairs . . . well, never mind. After a while I got up and staggered a few steps (the sun had zonked me), pretending to go to the bar but really so I could see her up close. A trickle of sweat ran down her rib cage onto her stomach. I went straight back to my room, bringing with me a tube of coconut oil, a product that I can't smell to this day without experiencing a kind of erotic dread.

I took the hotel bus into town after lunch, bought the usual junk, even explored a local hardware store, hammers, ladders. I felt as if I were looking for something, but I didn't have a clue what. And then suddenly I was sleepy, so sleepy I couldn't wait for the bus but took a taxi back to the hotel and stumbled to my room.

I collapsed on my bed. I turned the air conditioner on full blast. I read Georges Simenon for a few minutes, then rolled over and scrunched down in the cool air. I closed my eyes. I thought about this and that, but gradually I began to notice a strange smell issuing from my pillow. Still, I was happy and comfy and sailing downwards when the clanking began. I could feel myself waking up. I yanked open the French doors and looked down. Sure enough the air conditioner on the floor below had started up again. I looked to my right and left: there were rows upon rows of air conditioners, all humming and dripping in a quiet, civilized manner. How perfect that the only person in the hotel who truly needed his rest (that business with the dogs had put quite the strain on my system) was the *only* person who was going to be deprived of rest. I lay on my bed listening for a while longer, but then, in a spasm of anger, I leapt up with a curse, thrust myself into a pair of shorts—Lord, I was putting on weight!—and went outside into the blinding sunlight.

The tiles were scorching hot, so I walked very briskly to the ground floor and hotfooted it around back of the hotel, making my way over the stinging grass until I spotted my red bath towel hanging on a balcony. And there, below it, was the offending air conditioner. It seemed a rather beat-up thing, missing teeth in the protective grate while inside the blade whirred and clanked. I looked for an outside wire to cut. Nothing. I daydreamed about throwing a ski pole into the works, but where might I find a ski pole in this climate? I approached the wall. Even if I climbed onto the balcony railing of the first-floor room (which might well get me shot as a thief), I still couldn't reach the machine.

It was a puzzler, and I came back to my room to think about it. It seemed unsolvable. Finally, near dinnertime, soaked in sweat, my face red as a beet, I knocked on the door of the room below. A blond man, very tanned, answered. He was wearing one of those disgusting thong bathing suits. I could see his mahogany brown wife in the background.

"Excuse me," I said. I introduced myself, shook hands and explained about the air conditioner, about the racket it was causing.

He squinted at me. "But vee must have zee cold air."

Yes, well, that's true, I said with a laugh, an indulgent laugh, but you see it's ruining my holiday because I can't sleep. He called his mate over, meaty brown legs, also in a thong, her sandals making a sucking noise on the tiles. He said something to her in German. She replied with a wide-eyed shrug.

"Vee must have zee cold air," he repeated sorrowfully.

I thanked them. Germans never understand diplomacy, the Baader-Meinhof kids got that right, and I went back to my room. For a while I lay there, staring at the ceiling. Then, hearing a swish, I got up and looked for the source of the noise. Someone had slipped a handbill under my door. There, in five languages, was an announcement, a cabaret in the dining room tonight, all guests invited. Of course I wouldn't be able to go, I'd be too exhausted. I sat on the side of my bed and thought some rather lugubrious thoughts, *clank*, *clank* in the background. Then suddenly it stopped. The Krauts had left their room.

I nipped out on the front balcony and looked over. Yes, there they were, clip-clopping to the bar for an early drink. I looked at my watch. Seven o'clock. You've given them fair warning, I thought, that's all one can expect in this life. Fair warning. I put on a shirt and my moneybelt and went down to the lobby and flagged a taxi. He drove me into town, ten miles. I knew he was going to overcharge me, but I saw it all now as a necessary expense. Arriving in the main street, I had him drop me off at the hardware store, open till eight, thank you, and asked him to please wait while I shopped. I bought a large plastic tube of wood glue—it was right by the front door, a good omen—and a small portable ladder I'd seen that afternoon. Fifty dollars U.S. for both. Still cheaper than moving hotels. I threw the ladder into the trunk of the car (held down by a hunk of wire) and returned to the hotel.

After dark you could hear the excitement on the other side of the hotel, the guests milling about for the cabaret, perfumed and expensively dressed. Just before the first song went up, "Cabaret" (how perfect), the Krauts left their room downstairs. The light clicked off; the air conditioner stopped. I waited ten minutes, just to be sure they hadn't forgotten something, cock ring or nipple pincers, whatever, and then, taking my ladder, I hurried down to the ground floor and around to the back of the hotel, located my red towel and leaned the ladder against the wall. I measured the distance with my eye. It was perfect. The last step allowed me to reach the bottom of the air conditioner. Then, very quickly (time was short), I ran full speed back to my room. I pulled a pair of black dress socks from my suitcase, unfolded them over a day-old copy of *The New York Times* and soaked them in yellow glue.

I hurried back down to my ladder, sock in one hand, and climbed upwards. First things first. When I got to the top of the ladder, I placed my driver's licence on the top of the air conditioner. That way, if spotted, I could claim to have borrowed a house ladder to retrieve my driver's licence, which had fluttered out of my hand on the upstairs balcony and landed, lo and behold, on the top of their air conditioner. Then, parting the broken teeth, I stuffed the glue-soaked sock into the heart of the machine and wrapped it around the propeller. By now I was so excited I could feel the ladder shaking under me. I hurried back down, *clank, clank, clank*, scooped up the ladder, forgot my licence, put the ladder back, raced up the rungs, got my licence, and then brought the whole works back upstairs to my room. The whole business had taken less than three minutes.

I had a shower, ambled over to the cabaret. I didn't sit near the Germans but over at the side by myself. I may have had a bit too much to drink that night, because I can't quite remember leaving the patio. But I seemed to sober up as I climbed the stairs to my room. I came down the hall; I opened the door with an unsteady hand; I listened. Silence. I passed through the dark room and pushed open the doors. I heard the ocean, the wind, but nothing else. They weren't home yet. I lay on the bed and fell into a deep sleep.

Sometime later, near two in the morning, I heard a commotion downstairs and the outside light went on. I got up quietly and tiptoed over in the dark. There was a click, then another click. Then the sound of confused German. They were trying the air conditioner. Click, click, then silence. Then more clicks, then more German. Finally I crawled back into bed. I think I even laughed into the pillow so they couldn't hear.

Near three I woke up. I was itching like mad. I took a table fork and scratched the bottoms of my feet; they were on fire. I scratched and scratched. Then my scalp went off, then a patch on my back that I could only reach with my hairbrush. My pillow smelt funny. There must have been some kind of fungus in my room, a tropical fungus I was allergic to.

I went down to the main desk. It turned out they had an empty room; it had come free that night. Was this about the air conditioner, sir? No, this was another problem. They moved me. It was an identical room and I stood in the doorway, sniffing. I could smell that same musty air; my scalp started to itch. No good, I said. I went back to the desk. The night manager was called, an immaculate Spaniard with a toothbrush moustache. He listened to me carefully. He translated to his assistant. I heard the word *rojo*, three times. They must have been referring to my red face.

"I think you are allergic to the hotel," he said.

But I was exhausted, my scalp alive with red ants, the soles of my feet on fire, and in no mood to be trifled with. "Are you making fun of me?" I said.

He leaned forward with a patronizing smile. "I beg your pardon."

*"Est-ce que vous vous moquez de moi?"* I repeated with considerable force, going on to add that I was a respected professor of literature, that I didn't give a monkey's shit about the cost of things, that I wasn't going to remain on the premises an instant longer, and would he immediately arrange for another hotel. That seemed to turn the tide and very shortly he made me a proposition in exquisite French.

"Would you like to try one of our villas?" he asked. "They were built forty years before the main hotel, using different materials. You may find it more comfortable."

"At the same price?" I asked, my eyes involuntarily avoiding his.

He bowed gracefully. Moments later I was in a little golf cart, whisked to the pool end of the property, the moonlight dancing on the green water. The driver led me up the stairs to a sumptuous chateau and opened the door. I stepped inside. It was a two-floor affair, a television set, a living room, thick gold carpeting. The air smelt of salt and cleaning agents.

"Perfect," I said, and tipped the man five dollars.

But in the end the tropics are a depressing place, so sad, and after a few days, even in my lovely digs, I longed to go home. I wanted to wait a bit longer, let this business *avec les chiens* die down a bit. I didn't want problems, conversations with frowning neighbours, the police maybe.

The question is, though, what to do in the tropics? I didn't dare go near the pool: I knew I'd see the girl from the airplane there for sure, sunning herself and ruining my day. So I stayed in my room and read three consecutive Georges Simenon novels. Problem was, of course, within a few days I had exhausted my library, and a kind of nervousness set in as I finished off the final few pages of *Mémoires Intimes* before dinner. What would I do for the rest of the week? I ambled down to dinner, but because I was the only guest in the hotel without a family, entire tables looked away when I walked in, terrified, I think, that I might join them, that they might be stuck with me for the rest of the vacation.

Somewhere near nine I overhead a Dutch woman in the lobby telling someone there was a bookstore in another hotel a half-mile down the beach. I hurried along an illuminated flagstone path, moths darting here and there, anxious in case someone should get there before me and take the last good book. You can imagine my delight when, after spinning the book rotisserie, I came across *Monsieur Hire* on the bottom row, a Simenon I'd never read. But then I caught myself doing something rather odd: I *kept* looking. I looked at a John le Carré novel, I looked at a Tom Clancy novel, I even contemplated a biography of Perry Como. And in so doing I experienced the sudden conviction, as if I had just spotted a fault line in a cliff face, that I was never going to be happy, that I was, in fact, incapable of it; that I was doomed to spend the rest of my days doing precisely this, trying to improve on something that had, only moments before, seemed like the very embodiment of happiness itself.

To wit: A couple of nights later I smoked a joint on the beach with a wild-haired boy from Texas, and on the way back to my room it struck me that my time with Emma had been a kind of gorgeous treading water but that her *absence* (follow me here) provided, in itself, a kind of happiness because it gave me a precise object of desire, without actually giving me the thing itself, the ultimate possession of which could only diminish the pleasure that came from wanting it so unequivocally. It was a *pensée* so exhausting that I had to take a taxi into town immediately, where, sitting on a milk crate, I devoured an entire deep-fried fish, even the head.

The days passed slowly, symphonically, as they do when you're bored and lonely. Morning, afternoon, evening, three parts, all lasting far too long. At nightfall I had a strong rum drink in a bar down the beach to push away the haunted feeling that came over me every nightfall, the sense that the day was over, that there remained no more possibilities; that the store, so to speak, was closed till morning. Ahead lay a long night of twittering frogs and laughter from the pool (how isolating that sound is).

On my last night in town I put on a freshly laundered shirt and white slacks and a straw hat that suited me rather well and left the compound to have dinner at a well-known restaurant about fifteen miles away. It was a cliffside establishment, candles on the tables, the surf hissing below, *très intime*, and I sat at a small table near the edge. A full moon hung over the water.

I was there only a few minutes when a couple, dressed to the nines, he in a blazer, she in a shimmery blue dress, crossed the patio and sat at the table directly in front of me. It was the girl from the airplane. With her black hair brushed back, a touch of eyeliner, she looked so fantastic, so alluring in the candlelight—her eyes appeared black, her skin with a beauty mark on the collarbone—that for a second I considered cancelling my order. But I didn't and made a decision, for better or worse, to simply drink through it.

The table beside them cleared; a couple sat down, a stocky young man and his blonde wife; soon talk flew between the tables (how quickly people that age make friends!), laughter spilled up into the salty air . . . A story about a madman on the beach, a mix-up at the hotel check-in; a night in the mountains ("there was a rat, it was sitting on his *head*!"); lightning-fast ripostes (how fast they think, the sheer speed of it).

I ordered a fish dinner, red snapper. It took an hour, as it always does in the Caribbean, and by the time it arrived I was already drunk and had quite lost my appetite. I was thinking about Emma, that this gathering at the next table was precisely the kind of thing in which she had so often tried to include me, an evening with her friends. But they didn't interest me, to be honest. They weren't stupid, they were just too young, and I never went, not a wedding, not a dinner, not a party, not once in the whole three years.

"Would you like to join us?"

I looked around. It was the girl from the airplane.

"Me?" I said.

This provoked a volley of well-meaning laughter.

"Yes, you're all by yourself."

I picked up my drink. A waiter raced over as if I were in danger of toppling into the sea (perhaps I was) and, taking my glass, led me to their table. I sat down between her and her husband. Introductions were made ("My name is Jennifer and this is . . ."). I could smell her perfume.

"We've only been here two days," said the stocky young man, "but we're ready to leave already." That too set off another volley of laughter. After days and days of talking to myself, I felt quite giddy to have company and I laughed too.

Leaning forward abruptly, Jennifer started in on a story about growing up on Long Island, a father who read voraciously, a freckled boy at a dance. Her dress shimmered when she moved and I could see down her front. I had a feeling she knew it and knew I was looking and had had just enough to drink to find it cozily fine. Her voice, I noticed, had an odd tribble to it. That must be what Daisy Buchanan's voice sounded like, I thought.

Now the blonde woman took the floor. Suddenly we were in Tokyo. "We were on a game show. Everyone watched; they couldn't be*lieve* we could speak Japanese." She touched her husband's arm. "Or *he* could anyway. I was a few pounds heavier then and boy, did it ever show on television. I was never so embarrassed."

Her husband jumped in. "We couldn't get our modem to work over there. We ended up calling collect to New York, like *twelve* times! Finally they shipped us a new one—by courier. It was *wild*."

"Did you say something?" Jennifer whispered. The stocky young man was impersonating a Japanese bank manager.

In the tones of a gentleman making conversation (but, in fact, angling for exclusive attention), I said, "Actually, I was thinking about an old girlfriend."

"Was it a sad thought?"

"I was just thinking how much she would have enjoyed an evening like this."

"How come?"

"How come what?"

"How come she didn't enjoy an evening like this?"

"Because I didn't socialize with her. She was too young."

"Oh," she said, suddenly embarrassed.

"What?"

"Then *we* must seem rather young too."

Laughter rose up as the stocky man put a sandal to his ear like a telephone.

"No, you don't," I said. "And neither did she. Now that I think about it."

"But you like younger women?"

"I have to, really. The ones my age are all dead."

"I thought so," she said. She was fiddling with her spaghetti strap now, turning it between her finger and her thumb. Leaning forward.

"That all the women my age are dead? You really *thought* that?"

"You remind me a little bit of my father, actually. He prefers younger women too. That's how he says it. He says, 'I prefer young women, dear.'"

"You like your father?"

"Oh, terribly." Here a hand sought the back of her neck.

"What are you two talking about?" her husband asked, turning a handsome, open face to us.

"My father," she replied.

"Ah," he said diplomatically, and turned back to his conversation.

"They don't get along," Jennifer whispered.

Across the table the blonde woman had moved on to movies. "I just don't think he's a very good actor, that's all," she said, popping an ice cube into her mouth and crunching down loudly on it.

"Who?"

"Oh, what's his name? That *guy*. Christopher somebody."

"Christopher Walken?"

"That's him."

"You don't think Christopher *Walken* is a good actor?"

Jennifer returned her attention to me. "So you're here by yourself?"

"Yes."

"Seems like an odd place to come by yourself."

"I needed to get away."

"Woman trouble? That's another of my father's expressions."

"No, actually. I poisoned my neighbour's dogs."

After a moment she said, "How drunk are you?"

"Quite."

"Is that true?"

"What?"

"That you poisoned your neighbour's dogs."

"I'm afraid it is."

"*I* have dogs."

"Well, keep them away from me."

And on it went. We had more drinks, hard liquor this round, and after a while we left the restaurant, the five of us cramming into a taxi, women on men's laps, and drove into town. We ended up in a thumping second-floor discotheque near two in the morning. I went in the door and the bass hit me so hard in the chest that I wondered for a second if it was interfering with the rhythm of my heart. We sat around an absurdly small table in a dark corner. White rum and Cokes all around.

Leaning back in his chair, Jennifer's husband was watching the dance floor with something like amusement.

"Don't you dance, Professor?" he asked.

"Never," I said.

"Never?" shouted the stockbroker.

"Sometimes I *slow* dance," I said, but my words got lost in the smoke and the rolling bass line.

"What?" someone hollered across the table, frowning.

I cupped my hands over my mouth. "It's not worth repeating."

"I've heard people say that before," Jennifer's husband threw in. (Was he taking a turn for the sour?) "It means he wants someone to *ask* him to dance."

"Good heavens!" I protested.

"I'll slow dance with you, Professor," Jennifer said.

"Now?"

"Sure, why not?"

I didn't look at her husband as I got to my feet, but I thought I heard him shout a not very pleasant "Oh boy!" and clap his hands. I followed her past the front few couples and put my hand on her damp back.

"My husband is getting wrecked," she said. "This always happens on the last night of our holiday."

"No trouble, I hope."

"None worth talking about.

She slipped her cheek against mine and it seemed to me that she gave just the tiniest squiggle.

"Anyway," she said.

A couple banged into us. *Sorry, sorry.*

We danced on for a few moments and then I found myself coming to the gradual realization that I couldn't remember who I was dancing with. The white rum had taken a lethal step forward. I tried to *visualize* the face of the young woman with her head on my shoulder.

"What are you thinking about, Professor?" she asked. "You did a sort of change-up there."

"Nothing really."

"You must have been thinking about something. I could *feel* it."

I pulled back my head and looked at her.

"Oh," I said quietly. "It's you."

I heard her husband call out something. In a second he'd stagger onto the dance floor or she'd touch her temples and say, I don't feel well, I have to sit down.

"Listen," I said, "may I ask you something?"

"Sure."

"It's a little favour actually."

"What sort of favour?"

"Maybe not such a good idea after all."

"Say it, Professor."

"Okay then." It came out as if it were all one word. "Do you think it would be all right if I put my hand under your arm?"

She pulled back her head and frowned. "Under my arm? Like here?"

"Yes."

"It's pretty sweaty right there."

"I know."

She looked over at the table. Blurry pause. "Can you be discreet?"

I could feel the pressure of her hand on my back as she manoeuvred me out of the table's sightline. "Okay, go," she whispered.

I slipped my hand up the side of her ribcage.

"Did you get it?" she asked.

"Yes."

"Do I smell all right?"

"Yes. Great."

"What? What is it?"

"You smell like Emma," I said.

CHAPTER 7

*E*n tout cas. I was sitting in a café at the foot of my street, killing time before bed. Over the past few weeks I'd been organizing a book of essays on Arthur Rimbaud, but it was slow going. Several key contributors who had promised me papers had proven unreliable. One dropped out entirely, claiming he no longer believed his central thesis (that Rimbaud had not been a homosexual after all). No big loss there, but still it left a hole in the book, one which I was now obliged to fill with my own paper. Others were not up to scratch, obviously dashed off at the last moment, and I was in the delicate position of having to tell their authors that a complete overhaul was necessary. A woman at the university of Tel Aviv, who had been promising me her piece for months now, had taken to not replying to my urgent e-mails. My goodness, they were worse than undergraduates, and I was beginning to regret that I'd ever undertaken the project.

So that evening I found myself in a neighbourhood café. I liked the waiters there. Sometimes I went for a drink, and just a little chit-chat with one of them satisfied my hunger for a human voice or touch, and I could return home and resume my work without that hollowing sensation that I was living somehow on the margins of life.

I'd taken half a recreational sleeping pill and chased it with a pint of beer. Waiting for that certain flavour of burnt nuts to take hold, I picked up a local tabloid and while flipping through it noticed in the back a full three pages given to sex ads. Escort services, women who were men, a dominatrix named Sheeba, massage parlours. I'd seen this stuff before, but now I found it sort of disturbing. No, I'm being coy, it wasn't in the least disturbing. It was erotic.

Reading more closely, keeping an eye out for the waiter— I didn't want him to see me scrutinizing *de près* such material— I noted there was a massage parlour just down the street from where I was sitting. The Gold Hat Health Club. Odd, I'd never noticed it before. So I wrote down the phone number and, just for fun, or so I told myself, went over to the house phone on the bar and called the number.

Soft music came over the line and a girl's pleasant voice greeted me. I asked if they were open for business. "We are," she replied with a tone of barely suppressed high spirits, which for all its transparent commercial motivation made me feel *quand même* as if somehow she and I had struck up a strangely immediate rapport, as if she had recognized something (ahem) special in my voice.

I asked how late.

"Late," she said offhandedly, and the word seemed charged with implication, as if gumdrops hung suspended on its frame.

I went back to my table in an uneasy state. I had the sensation of sliding into a dark hole, like those nights years ago when, brushing my teeth in the bathroom, I caught myself daydreaming about Emma, about what was going to happen in a matter of minutes when I slipped into bed beside her delicious-smelling body.

I paid my bill and went over for a peek. It was a nondescript low-rise next door to a pharmacy. On the door, along with a list of doctors, income tax services for Portugal's newly arrived, even a night dentist, were the words The Gold Hat Health Club. Even the letters that spelt out this absurd name seemed charged and beckoning, a kind of, how shall I say, naughty come hither, provoking in me the fluttery stomach an adolescent might experience as he smuggles a girlie magazine past the parental living room. It was a sort of *black* excitement.

I went through the double glass doors and walked to the far wall, where a small elevator waited. The doors rolled open with a clang and I got in, pushing a button for the top floor. We lurched upwards, small square portals giving view to colourless hallways, before coming to a stop at level number three. A bear-shaped man, Slavic I assumed, and his bear-shaped wife (keep the Kalashnikov out of *her* hands) got in. They must have been the cleaning staff. The doors closed and we proceeded upwards. Realizing they were going up, not down, the man lurched forward, slapping the buttons with the heel of a meaty hand as if the carriage were whisking the three of us to our deaths. The wife, who was wearing a faded purple coat, looked at me with considerable embarrassment, although I thought I detected a hint of something else in her sympathetic features, as if she knew where I was going and wished me to know that while she understood my being a man and all, there was still something unattractive about it. It unnerved me, this glancing regard, because it made me feel as if I were carrying my soul on the outside of my body, the more easily to be bruised, even scarred.

I experienced a moment of short, stabbing doubt. Surely I should have done better than this with my life. Had I not scoffed at people like me in my early twenties? Felt sorry for them, ached for them, those middle-aged men talking too energetically to young women on a street corner or in a café. Yes I had, it's true, but those were unforgiving years. I had scoffed at *everything*. I had assumed in the privacy of my own darting thoughts that everyone wanted to be me but lacked the vigour, the courage, the élan. The only thing in common between those years and now, I observed unhappily, was a capacity on my part to find a persuasive explanation for anything I chose to do. In other words, viewed from my own eyes, I was seldom on the wrong team for very long.

The lurid draw of the ad in the back of the tabloid seemed a long way off now. Its spell had worn off like Novocaine, and I saw a discomfiting image of myself as a chinless dentist led by the nose into a Mexican brothel, where in the space of an hour I would be fleeced for several hundred dollars' worth of drinks for the señoritas, jacked off into a dirty washcloth and sent out the door minus my passport.

With a kind of numb dread I got out of the elevator on the fifth floor, the Russians staying on board, and I picked my way down a mucous-green hallway, passing the night dentist's office where a nurse sat in full view, door open, cap and whites on, watching with mild contempt all those who made their way to the Gold Hat Health Club.

I tapped my knuckles on suite 501 and as the door swished shut behind me I found myself in a dark, heavily carpeted foyer. Chocolate rugs, chocolate walls, wall hangings, paintings, all virtually indistinguishable under subdued track lighting. Latin pop music issued from invisible speakers. A large fish tank gurgled in the corner, in which one almost expected to see a human head, the hair swishing slowly back and forth like seaweed.

I was not alone long. A door opened and a tall young woman with a bony face and crimped hair emerged from a back room.

"Yes?" she said.

"Could I get a massage here?"

"Oh," she said, pleasantly surprised, and revealed a set of small pointed teeth. "Didn't I just speak to you on the phone?"

"Yes, that was me."

"You certainly got here fast."

"I wasn't far away."

"Have you been here before?"

"No, actually, I haven't."

"It's sixty-five dollars for a forty-five-minute workout. Plus any tip you might care to leave, of course."

*Workout?*

"Of course."

Opening a door on her right, she led me into a narrow hallway. A heavy musk hung in the air. She knocked softly on a door and went in. It was a small, immaculate room with drawn curtains and a linen-covered massage table at its centre.

"Is there anyone you'd like to see?" she asked with professional sunshine.

"What are my choices?"

"Well, there's Cindy, Minky, Sally." She paused coyly. "Or me, of course. I'm Wendy."

I looked at her long bare arms.

"Are you available?"

"I am."

"That would be lovely."

She smiled her pointy-toothed smile again. "I'll give you a few minutes to get yourself ready."

The door shut and I was alone again. I took off my clothes and laid them neatly on a chair, like a schoolboy. I looked around for a towel, something to wrap myself with, but there was nothing, just a small nightstand at the head of the table with a box of Kleenex, a can of baby powder and a large bottle of baby oil. I lay on my stomach on the table, but not without first examining the sheet for unsavoury stains. There were none, not that I could make out much; it was very dark in there. I must have been nervous, I could smell myself. Well, not exactly myself. This was the second time it had happened. I smelt like Emma. That sharp, almost frightened animal smell came out from under my arms. I sniffed again. By now the whole room smelt of her.

The door opened and I jumped.

"Would you like oil or baby powder?" Wendy asked. She was wearing a pair of fluttery black trousers, imitation silk, and a matching sleeveless top.

"Which would you recommend?"

"Some customers like the oil; others like the powder." Seeing the uncertainty on my face, she continued, "We could start with the baby powder and save the oil till the end."

So she began. I lay on my stomach and for the longest time her hands moved over my back, my neck and shoulders. I began to have the rather anxious concern that perhaps I'd made a mistake, that I might end up with nothing more than a, well, a massage. But why, I wondered, was she wearing that black sleeveless outfit? Surely professionals wore something more, I don't know, appropriate. Her hands fluttered down to my buttocks. The brush of her fingernails made my skin rise with goosebumps. She moved lower and, while touching the inside of my leg, brushed ever so slightly a part of me that remains *hors de combat* in a regular massage. Was it an accident? I didn't know, and the not knowing gave things an aura of titillating suspense. Her fingers whisked along the backs of my legs; they slipped around the side and ran up the inside of my thigh like a tarantula. It happened again and I let out an affected moan, more of a hint really, more of a *You're getting warmer* signpost than a spasm of pleasure. I shifted my hips to make a necessary adjustment and observed that she waited with professional élan while things were being rearranged.

"Perhaps you'd be more comfortable if you rolled over," she said. I did.

"Oh!" she said with practised surprise, catching sight of me. "You must know what comes next."

"Not exactly."

"Would you care for a hand release?"

*A hand release.*

"I'm not sure. Would I?"

"You've been here before?"

"No, I told you."

"But you've been to places *like* this before?"

"Well, I've had a massage before."

"Never mind," she said. "Just close your eyes."

I heard her move to the top of the table and then return. There was a squishing sound and her warm, slippery hand embraced me. She then executed a hand release, not a wasted stroke, which left me half sitting, my fists clenched to my temples.

After a moment I eased myself back down. Not knowing what to say (what *does* one say?), I said, "That was excellent."

And then she did an extraordinary thing. She leaned over and kissed me on the cheek. Slippery as an eel, still seeing stars, I stared at the ceiling while she went down the hall to fetch a hot cloth. I felt immeasurably better, as if a transfusion of bright red, highly oxygenated blood had been injected into my body. Better still, the smell was gone, Emma's smell, replaced by the rather thick, cloying scent of baby oil that would later make my trousers feel as if they were sticking ever so vaguely to my skin.

Out on the street the night seemed brighter, the people lissom. I checked my watch and was indifferent to find that my long-armed friend with the beautiful touch had had me in and out of there in twenty minutes and still managed a twenty-dollar tip.

In front of me a young girl with a violin case walked along the sidewalk, her hair moving with the motion of her body. Such a graceful waist, such soft brown hair still streaked by the sun or lemon juice or perhaps by youth alone. At the corner, as if sensing the presence of something behind her, she looked quickly over her shoulder. Freckled cheekbones, green eyes. It was a lovely image, and I could look at it, admire it, without feeling despair at knowing I could never have her. I felt, for the next hour or so anyway, free not just from desire but, more important, from the *worry* that that desire would not be fulfilled.

So it began. I became a regular at the Gold Hat, turning up on Thursday nights for "a rub and a tug," as the girls called it, right after my evening lecture (we had moved on to Molière by now). It was not an uncomplicated experience for me. Sometimes, hurrying along the street, I'd find myself thinking about Emma, about our final months together. I confess now that I made love to her every day I lived with her but even more, way more, near the end, when I felt the noose tightening around my throat, when I felt her young soul moving away from me. And as she withdrew, it was suddenly

I who became the talker, who made the obscene requests, the memories of which can still make me blanch. I was like a rabbit in that sense, not the fraternity-joke rabbit but rather the rabbit with no memory. I seemed to have no *accumulated* familiarity with Emma's body. I never got used to fucking her. When I smelt her in a movie or browsing through a store after dinner, it was as if my sexual memory of her had been wiped clean like a blackboard with a damp rag and her body was fresh and narcotically new to me again.

But I wondered now about those mornings when I had pinned her thin wrists to the headboard at the crack of dawn. Perhaps it had all been a bit much for her, a bit *gross* really, as if she were submitting to something. Perhaps her haste to get out of bed wasn't always a hunger for an early start to the day but rather to avoid getting pumped by a soft-bodied, middle-aged man, who in the aftermath fell back to sleep like a drugged animal while she tiptoed about the house, trying not to rattle cutlery or drop the toilet seat lest she awake *monsieur* from his slumbers.

Anyway, I'd catch myself thinking about this sort of thing as I neared my appointment *avec les demoiselles*; curious, distracting thoughts, almost as if I were trying to wreck it for myself, this simple, straightforward pleasure.

Let me backtrack. Midway through my Thursday-night lecture on *Le Médecin malgré lui*, I would find myself daydreaming about the evening ahead, about the bare-breasted girl, her cotton dress unbuttoned at my request, standing beside me at the massage table.

"May I touch you there?" I'd say.

"If you want." They talked to you in a quiet, soothing voice, those girls.

"Or there?"

"I'm not supposed to, but okay."

Anticipating this scenario, I would find myself dizzy and somewhat distracted at the front of my class. *Yes*, I pointed out to my students, *Molière was an early champion of women and you can see that in* . . . And sometimes I'd drift off, jaw slightly open while the hushed class waited for me to toss a fresh fish into the net. Other times just thinking about those baby-oil girls made me crave a cigarette as one might after witnessing a bank robbery. But I never indulged myself. At my age a cigarette de-sexes you, as if the blood is cut short to your groin, is bumped onto a shorter, shallower track.

It was February now. A hard cold lay on the streets; smoke rose from chimneys in blue puffs that hung momentarily in the air and then scattered quickly, chilled and impatient to get away. The city was locked in a vise. In that terrible stillness you felt somehow in danger, like Napoleon's men trudging back from Moscow.

Concluding my lecture, I fled the building, deferring until "later" the after-class discussion that I had myself suggested. The nasal-voiced geek with the prominent Adam's apple, the untidy girl with the troublesome landlord, the blue-jeaned baby who'd do anything for an A ("Have you thought of *studying*, Angie?")—it all fell from my shoulders as I raced through the exit doors. I hurried as if I might miss something, as if there was a terrible urgency. What if the large-breasted Janie was already with a client? Or green-eyed

Margie was playing hooky again? By the time I reached Bloor Street, my stomach was in a knot. I was like a famished man who has settled down at a feast only to suspect someone is going to snatch away his plate.

I hurried along the street, a gloved hand covering my mouth and cheeks, past the Medical Arts Building, the Faculty of Education, the health food store. But in the act of crossing Spadina, I noticed that something had changed. I was no longer driven by the same excitement. Somewhere back there the desire had slipped away, vanished into the cold air. My brain fussed and jumped with irrelevant concerns: money, my mortgage, a slight at work, a student who dropped my doctoral seminar for Serrault's. Like an ecstatically planned vacation that, as it approaches, seems somehow to lose the very magic that inspired it in the first place, the closer I got to the massage parlour, the less compelling, the more pedestrian, even sordid the whole thing seemed. Where had they gone, those stomach-plunging fantasies, now that I was almost on top of the place where they could be realized? What was this debris floating like junk in my head? What had happened in those blocks between Molière and Spadina?

I arrived at the door to the low-rise and hesitated. There didn't seem any *point* now. The spell, the fit, whatever it was that had afflicted me like a flu bug in the lecture hall, appeared to have passed. But I knew that if I turned around and went home empty-handed, so to speak, it would all start up again. The green-eyed girl with the open dress would gather heat and urgency in my imagination in direct proportion to the distance I moved away from her.

I got out of the elevator and moved along the hallway as if on wheels, the thick scent of baby oil hanging in the air. I went in without knocking; the fish tank gurgled soundlessly; the hostess emerged; I kissed her on both cheeks, *à la française*; I went down the hall to my usual room, took off my clothes, peeped naked through the blinds. Outside on the street, people passed to and fro, hunched in the cold, toques and scarves and long coats hurrying back and forth under the window. Somewhere out there, ten blocks away maybe, I imagined Emma in her kitchen; she was straightening a magnet on the fridge while she talked on the telephone. But why would I think about that now? It was perverse, as if my own imagination were throwing chairs in my path . . .

There was a knock at the door. I sat down quickly and rested my hands in my lap. It was Margie. Green-eyed Margie in a green dress.

"Oil or powder, Professor?"

Sometimes, if it was a slow night, I stayed on for a bit, had a cigarette with the girl. They were mostly single mothers. We talked about babysitters and daycare centres, bad husbands and going straight. They all wanted to go straight, and some did. It was a surprise. You'd go to the dentist and he'd introduce you to his new receptionist and it'd be Binky, who'd charged you eighty dollars for a slide. (That's when they oil themselves up and slide up and down your body.) Or you'd be going through Customs at the airport and when you looked up from your open suitcase, it'd be Passion going through your underwear. As if she hadn't seen it before, folded neatly on top of your clothes on a chair.

CHAPTER 8

A word or two about Passion, if I might.

It was a Monday night and I took the long route home. I'd had a nap in the afternoon that had left me splendidly refreshed. I was eager to do something and rather hoped to run into a friend, a colleague, someone to have a drink with. The weather was still cold. Women pushed by, their faces buried in their coats, sometimes holding scarves to their mouths and looking worried or angry. Turning up Euclid Avenue, I thought I might drop in on Serrault. He and his boyfriend had a house at the top of the street and, although one normally doesn't drop in on a Frenchman, I had a morsel of gossip for him. The wife of a colleague whom we both despised had run off with a rather famous clown from a German circus. Serrault was partial to circuses, I knew that. He'd written a book about them, *Vers le langage des clowns: Étude sémiotique,* and when he was a young man in France, after securing his *maîtrise,* he had worked as an assistant to a legendary lion tamer, cleaning cages, feeding the animals and so on. Later (and here I'm telling stories out of school), Serrault had tried to create a Canadian circus, borrowing here and there, even from the faculty. The enterprise had ended in debacle, leaving him with a debt that took a decade to pay off but also with a bear, which for a period of weeks dwelt in his garage. This same four-hundred-pound animal he walked late at night through one of the city's more affluent neighbourhoods on the end of a chain.

I knocked on the door of his flat, but there was no response. I went to the front window to see if I could catch a glimpse of him through a split in the curtains, which I did, for there was M. Serrault dancing in the middle of his living room, not wildly or lewdly but rather playfully, his tie slightly loosened. I gather his companion was in the room, perhaps just under the window frame, because he appeared to be addressing someone. He danced well, and he knew it, his torso quite still, his narrow hips moving gracefully, but there was a disarming casualness to it, a throwaway self-deprecation that one wouldn't have suspected from so rigorous an intellect. (Indeed, he was becoming quite famous.) I stood at the window watching a moment longer, but some things one does not interrupt and so I slipped back out to the street, leaving Serrault dancing under the winter moon.

Returning the way I came, I found myself feeling oddly comforted, as if I had just had a social encounter and could now return to my house and my book (another Elmore Leonard, I'm afraid) with a clean conscience. A life lived with sufficient fullness and so on. In fact I felt a small surge of pleasure when I realized I still had a hundred pages to go.

It was near the bottom of the street that I noticed a one-storey brick building on my right. The Village Health Spa. I could see activity inside, the lights were on, a television flickered. I checked my watch. It was ten o'clock.

With a cigarette in the corner of his mouth and a wall eye, the man at the reception desk looked like a seedy Jean-Paul Sartre. He seemed surprised to see me, although with that face he could have been suspicious or guilty or venal; I couldn't tell. But *louche*, like that wandering eyeball.

"Are you open?" I asked.

"Yes," he said.

An American sitcom was playing on the television set in the adjoining foyer, and its aggravating laugh track, *ha-ha-ha*, *ha-ha-ha*, complemented the junky tones of the place, like something one might find on a tray of tin foil. A black girl emerged from a back room. She was attractive, but there was something not quite right about her mouth, as if her top lip had been split open and had healed badly. She was self-conscious about it too, covering her mouth reflexively when she saw me, and her shyness drew me to her. I noticed also that she was wearing the same leather bikini, complete with fringes, that I'd seen on Binky at the other place. There must have been a sale on them. She plopped herself on the chesterfield and swept up a magazine. I was on the verge of fleeing—the establishment was notches below par—when I smelt that strange sex pollen, the mildly sickening bouquet of baby oil, which had acquired a kind of Pavlovian appeal for me.

"Are you available?" I asked.

"Sure."

"Dr. Scobie," I said, extending my hand.

"I'm Passion," she said with a trace of amusement. Of course that wasn't her name. It was an absurd choice, a sort of chronic masturbator's daydream of a name, and she knew it.

It was a small enterprise, only two tables in the back. Not very clean either. I caught sight of a ball of crumpled toilet paper on the floor beside the massage table, semen-soaked, I imagined, from a previous client. Passion bent over with a swish of leather and fringes and swept it up. A wooden statue stood glowering in the corner. It was an Indian chief, human size, in full war paint and headdress.

"And what's this?" I asked.

"Oh, *him*," she said. "Someone stole his tomahawk."

It was true. In a raised fist there was an unoccupied hole in which it had once perched.

"Now *who* would steal a tomahawk?" I asked.

"Stick around," she said, and then with the weariness of a waitress at the end of a long shift she outlined my options: regular, topless, bottomless, nude reverse ("that's where you do me") or a slide.

I took the regular.

"Oil or powder?" she asked.

I replied. "Powder. At first."

I won't include all the things the Indian saw, but I will say that after I had given her my credit card and she had disappeared from the room to return with a steaming hot face cloth, after all those pleasant formalities, we remained in the cubbyhole, chatting. She had a dirty, funny mouth and the loyalty of a prostitute. She spared no details about her customers: the Greek with the stubby member ("it was like a cucumber") who never tipped; a local actor; a police detective; a housewife who liked to watch her husband. Some liked their bums paddled, their nipples tweaked; some sniffed her linen; some required a medical inspection, some a mild bawling-out; for some, only a good smack in the chops would do the job. But if they tipped, they were okay. Rule of thumb was, the bigger the pervert, the bigger the tip. I had a sense of having heard all these stories before but enjoyed the fact of her telling me, the confidence. Thinking back on it, I must have been lonelier than I realized, but the truth is that I have a warm memory of that evening and its aftermath, the two of us smoking cigarettes and gabbing. When I left, I felt clear-headed and energetic and quite ready for a lecture preparation, a read, a drink at the corner, whatever the evening might afford me. It seemed like gravy now. On the way home I talked to myself in French, something I always do when I'm happy.

I went back to see Passion only a few days later and the same delicious ritual ensued. But this time, as I was giving her my charge card, I asked her a question. "How much of this do you get to keep?"

"The tips," she said.

"What if you don't get a tip?"

"Then I get fifteen bucks."

"On a sixty-five-dollar massage?"

"Yep."

She liked the feel of where this was going. I sat back down on the table.

"I have a proposition for you," I said.

"Oh yes?"

"I'm suggesting that perhaps we could cut out the middleman entirely."

She looked at me suspiciously.

"Let's say, for the sake of argument, that you were to come to my house . . ."

"I'm not sure about that."

"Hang on. You come to my house, you give me a massage there, but you get to keep all the money."

"That's against house rules."

"We wouldn't tell anyone. It would be a private arrangement between you and me."

"I don't know," she said, but you could see a shard of venality glint in her eye. "Are you a cop?"

"Do I look like a cop?"

"An old one."

"I'll tell you what I'll do," I said. "I'll give you my name and my phone number and you can think about it. How's that?"

"You live nearby?"

"Just up the street." I handed her my card. She examined it. "My name's not really Dr. Scobie."

"What do you teach?" she asked.

"French literature."

You could see her mind shuffling strange cards into a new hand. She removed the undersheet from the massage table and, taking a spray bottle from the nightstand, gave it a couple of squirts and dried off the plastic with the soiled sheet.

"All right, Professor," she said. "I'll think about it."

Several days went by during which I was unusually busy. A visiting professor from the University of Rennes delivered a good paper on Verlaine; nothing groundbreaking, but I liked the way he told us what we all already knew. I took him to dinner afterwards and we consumed a number of bottles of wine, after which the conversation turned, of course, to women. It still strikes me as curious that men talk of virtually nothing else.

The following morning I was slightly ill and neglected to eat breakfast. By mid-afternoon I was starving, I had a raging headache and, after a student seminar on Boileau, I intended to rush home and get something to eat. The paper was presented by a young girl with a sort of Cleopatra hairdo. Short bangs, long at the back. She was Russian, I think, for I detected just a dusting of an accent. I had to remind her several times to address the class, not me, but when she did, she revealed a profile that was almost unbearably beautiful. I wanted to reach over and touch her neck, to feel her skin, which was so soft, I imagined, that it would be like putting one's fingers in a bowl of cream. And yet I noticed that when she faced me front-on the effect was diminished somewhat, and I felt the relief that you experience sometimes when you find a flaw in a too gorgeous woman.

Still, after the seminar I meandered slowly down the front steps of the university with the ridiculous hope that she might be there, waiting for me. But she wasn't. I saw her riding her bicycle up the middle of the snowy street. I wanted to call out for her to be careful, but it was too transparent.

I suddenly remembered how hungry I was. It would take too long to go home and cook a meal, so I stopped off at a large grocery store in the Manulife building to pick up a heated roast beef sandwich. I was so famished, I think I would have gunned my way to the food counter if necessary. I was rushing across the floor—I had just passed a rack of barbecue chickens, the smell from which made me even more impatient—when I looked up and saw Emma Carpenter. She was standing by a fruit tray, an orange in her hand, and she appeared to be discussing the orange with a tall, angular-featured man. A face that could wear hats.

I broke stride for a moment. It had, after all, been more than a year since I'd seen Emma. Sensing some arrhythmic movement in the room, she looked up. And *recoiled*. There's no other way to describe it. It was as if someone had thrown a glass of water on a cat. She edged closer to her companion, like a child stepping behind a parent. It was all quite involuntary, and that's what made it so shocking. It was as if she had encountered a man who had beaten her or raped her, as if her body had remembered *on its own* an assault and had responded intuitively. My God, I thought, so *that's* what she thinks of me. And yet—I don't know how to say this without sounding pathological—the notion that Emma thought of me at all was something of a comfort. You see, *my* body remembered too.

In any event I ran into Serrault on the street shortly afterwards. He was shopping for a meat thermometer (he was quite the cook) and, to his surprise and mine, I began to tell him about this odd sighting of Emma. Midway through it my heart began to pound and a sensation of *thinness* overcame me, as if I were somehow lying, as if I were suggesting that the sheer violence of her response implied that she was somehow still in love with me. It got worse. Describing my reaction to her, namely, walking out of the store *sans rien dire*, without even a nod, I seemed to be suggesting, however coyly, that while it was she who had abandoned me, it was now *I* who kept the door locked. I kept on. I insisted, my voice almost an octave higher now, that sometimes it made me even *happy* to think about her, to bathe in the knowledge that I had, in fact, recovered. Totally. But the more I tried to explain all this, the more self-deluding, the more obsessed I sounded. (Even now I feel a tad too insistent.) By the end of it I felt as if my body had been poisoned, and I was in a foul mood.

Serrault, of course, had no response whatsoever except for mild sympathy. "*Tiens*," he said, and ducked into a kitchen supply shop. A turkey baster had caught his eye.

That evening I sat out on the back patio in a coat and hat, smoking cigarettes and staring into the garden. And after a while I remembered, *comme ça*, a picture of Emma rushing down the basement stairs with a load of laundry. Why that image? I don't know. It's just that there was something slightly sad about it, as if somehow I should have put my arms around her to stop that nervous rushing, that agitated way of being. She behaved sometimes, I now recalled, like a kid afraid of "getting in heck." I think she may even have used that phrase once. *Getting in heck.*

Suddenly my ears began to buzz and I had the feeling that I had entered into her thoughts as sure as if I had put my hand through the wall of her chest and clutched her heart.

The garden hung in frozen icicles; they gleamed under the yard lights. I dropped my cigarette, and when I leaned over to pick it up I exhaled a gust of frozen breath that darted away like a thought. I exhaled again and could see the momentary shapes of an island, a boat, a field, even Brazil. My imagination was like an independent living thing, like a reef or the earth itself. And in one of these exhalations I saw with the detail of a well-lit film the image of Emma walking along a wintry street. She was talking with great animation to a short, grey-haired man. I'd never seen him before, but at one point she stopped dead in her tracks and turned to him and said, I'm so *happy!*

It was as if her soul was speaking to me, to my soul, as if she were saying, *Stop thinking about me. Please. Leave me alone.*

I was still rocky the next day—at my age hangovers are two-day affairs—but I had a number of administrative meetings to attend.

University departments are run by dictators who surround themselves with committees; it gives things the aura of democracy, and you have to turn up. There was a full afternoon with the Course Content Committee, which provided an opportunity for new faculty members (those without tenure) to second-guess the pleasures of department head Camille Dupré.

Let me say off the top that Dupré was not the college's first choice. That went to a Harvard man, a white-haired gentleman with an international reputation (Montaigne). We were thrilled to steal him away (and only five years from retirement, no less). But during orientation week there was an incident. To put it mildly. He went to a local pub with a bunch of freshmen and at closing time invited the group back to his rented house on the Toronto campus. More drinking ensued, the hour got late and students drifted off home, until there was only one left, a strawberry-haired boy from Manitoulin Island. The young man, fresh to the city, had drunk considerably more than he could hold, a situation the learned professor handled by stripping him naked, fucking him in the ass and then pissing on him.

After that Dupré looked like a positive *catch*. He was a consummate second-rater; everyone knew it. After twenty-eight years in North America he rigorously maintained the affectation of barely speaking English. All shrugs and pouts he was, traits that made him seem like "the real thing" in our community. In the staff lounge he made a great show of shuffling through the papers in his briefcase, ordering and reordering them into fresh stacks, as if some great activity were in full flight. Serrault, of course, despised him; thought he was a joke as a scholar, a decade "behind the coup," as he put it. One day he caught me laughing perhaps too heartily at one of Dupré's modest asides and quickly lowered his eyes. It made my cheeks flush with embarrassment for precisely the reason that Serrault had tried to hide it from me. He was a complicated man, but the spectre of human abasement, no matter how passing, was not among his pleasures.

There were other matters to attend to as well. The Standards Committee had been called into emergency session. A fourth-year student had somehow slipped through the net and all but secured his undergraduate degree by taking twenty *first-year* courses. He'd taken them at various colleges and skilfully muddied his tracks. It was the *Alice's Restaurant* approach, a strategy we'd been aware of since the late seventies. How did it happen? Whose responsibility was it? Should the student be denied his degree because of administrative incompetence? The meeting droned on into the evening, Serrault, naturally, taking the student's side and alienating, as always, a portion of the faculty with the crisp observation that the difference between a fourth-year and a first-year course was negligible.

"Speak for yourself," Dupré said with a wintry smile.

"I am," replied Serrault, and shrugged his shoulders. One wants to cheer at those moments. Self-deprecation among the gifted leaves me breathless with admiration.

It was well after ten at night when I got home. I poured myself a glass of wine and lay down on the couch in my study. Looking at my desk littered with papers, pencils, correspondence, academic journals, memos stuck to the computer, I felt a tingle of curious pleasure. Then the phone rang.

It was Passion. She was downtown for the evening. Perhaps I wanted to get together. Yes, I said, that would be splendid. It had rather the aura of a date. Twenty minutes later she got out of a taxi in front of my house with a large handbag. Very large indeed. She came inside and looked at my bookshelves with a show of appreciation. It struck a slightly false note.

It was odd to see each other outside our usual context, a bit like running into a high school teacher during summer vacation.

"I don't have my stuff," she said, and touched the narrow white scar under her nose.

"That's all right."

"Do you want to do it here? On the couch?"

"It's a bit exposed," I said. "What do you normally do?"

"I don't normally make house calls." Again the hand to the lip.

I went to the bottom kitchen drawer and shuffled about in the party napkins and stray forks and bits of string until I found a black candle. It had been a while since I'd entertained anyone. I set it in Emma's bronze candlestick, lit the wick and turned out the lights. The melting wax gave off a scent of black cherries.

"That smells nice," Passion said, meaning, I think, that she liked the candlelight better. In the shadows she looked quite lovely, and I realized I had never had a black woman in my house before.

"Are you comfortable?"

"Yes. You?"

"I'm asking because you said you never do this."

"You never know," she said.

"But this time you did."

"You seem okay," she said. "I knew that much."

We sat for a moment in silence.

"How's your time?" I asked.

She looked at her watch. "I have a friend coming to get me at midnight. Can I smoke in here?"

"Certainly." I got up to get her an ashtray.

She lit a cigarette and exhaled the smoke in my direction.

"How's the wine?" I asked.

"It tastes like blood."

I took a taste. It was a Merlot, with an excellent bouquet, but she was right: it seemed to have come from the throat of a butchered animal.

I also noticed that I was getting a bit drunk, that things were starting to assume a sort of new and convincing order; as if I'd stepped into a movie, *in medias res*, and accepted, from the moment of entry, the logic of the story. What story? I'll get to that. Suffice it to say that over the past six or seven months I had caught myself slipping rather quickly into a dreamy world where ideas occurred to me that were not at all appropriate. Comments I should make to colleagues, subjects for academic scrutiny. Sometimes I wrote them down and the following morning, when I deciphered the handwriting, they seemed, at best, rather thin, at worst (and more and more frequently) touched by a kind of insane sparkle. I have long learned to stay away from the telephone when drunk, but the world has changed and I confess that some mornings I have woken up and dashed to my computer to check that the previous evening, while caught up in one of these "stories," I had not composed an imprudent communication to a woman or a friend or a student. I hadn't made a slip so far, but it worried me. I feared that one of these nights I would drink *too long*. I want you to know that I saw the seeds sprouting early on; I knew those vines when they were like little snakes just stirring in a warm nest.

But I'm digressing, as I do more frequently these days. My memory, like my concentration, seems to be disintegrating like wet toilet paper.

"We should get started," I said to Passion. "Would the bedroom be all right?"

"Sure. Do you want to take a shower first?"

I left her in the living room and went into the bathroom and undressed and turned on the shower and got under the hot water. I was quite excited. The evening, painted crimson now by the wine, had a compelling, adventurous quality to it. I don't know how long I was under the shower. I know that afterwards, dripping wet, I tried to take a pee and stood there, God knows how long, staring into the toilet bowl, thinking about God knows what.

I came out in my dressing gown, a floor-length bath towel affair that Emma had bought me for Christmas. Taking the candle in hand, I led Passion rather unsteadily into my bedroom. I turned down the bed, the top sheet, dropped the bathrobe to the floor and lay down on my stomach. I heard the sound of shoes being removed, then a brush of material, and when I looked over my shoulder I saw that she had removed her shirt and was wearing a white brassiere and jeans.

"You might as well get the works," she said.

"I've never been with a black woman before."

I heard her laugh. "I wouldn't exactly call this being with a black woman." She put her hands on my back.

"You have a beautiful touch," I said.

"Uh-huh."

"No, really."

"Good. I'm glad."

"Can I roll over?"

"It's your house."

"Can you take that off?"

She undid her brassiere and her breasts with their large dark nipples came free. She put her hands on her hips. "Do you want me to do your chest?" she asked.

"Sure."

"And then your legs?"

"Sure."

"And then we'll see what happens."

She didn't cover her mouth.

"You're quite beautiful," I said.

"And I can't believe you're sixty years old."

"I'm not."

"You told me you were."

"I'm fifty-four."

"Why do you tell people you're sixty?"

"I like the sound of it."

"Do you want me to do your legs now?"

"Yes."

"Tops, or bottoms?"

"Tops please." My voice wobbled.

"Like that?"

"Yes, that's great."

"They feel a bit tight."

"They are."

It was silent for a while.

"You should open them up a bit."

I shifted position.

"How's that?" she said.

"Fabulous." I covered my eyes.

"Don't go to sleep on me."

"Don't worry."

After a while she said, "Do you have any cream?"

"Ah, no."

"My hands are dry."

"That's all right."

She stopped for a second, spat into her palm and put her hand back on me. "I hope you don't mind," she said. "Is that all right?"

"That's fine."

"You're sure? Some guys are squeamish."

"Shhh."

"My, my," she said after a moment, and sat back. "My, my."

I opened my eyes. She sat motionless, her hands open like a surgeon waiting for his gloves to be put on.

"Are you feeling all right?"

"Fine," I said, "lovely."

"Do you have any Kleenex?"

I pointed her down the hall. In a little while I heard the door close; that distinct rattle of the toilet-paper roller rolling over; the toilet flushing; then a sound I couldn't place immediately, a sort of clank. A few moments later she returned, quite comfortable, it seemed, to meander about my house half naked, which rather flattered me.

"Would you care to go out and get something to eat?" I asked.

"Are you hungry or something? You're supposed to be sleepy and relaxed."

"I'm not, though. I'm famished."

She hesitated. "I didn't bring any money."

"It'll be my treat. But what about your friend?"

"I don't have a friend coming. I just wanted to make sure you weren't a pervert."

Feeling more wide awake than I had for months, as if I could blister paint on a wall just by looking at it, I got up and got dressed.

"Oh," I said as we were leaving, "your bag."

"I'll get it when I come back."

It was after eleven by now. The floodlights had long since been turned off on the skating rink, but there were still a couple of kids out there, soaring around in the dark, and you could hear the sound of their skates hacking into the ice in short, excited strokes. Passion, wearing an imitation red leather coat with a fur collar, walked with her head down, her hands in her pockets. It seemed as if the sound of our footsteps made us both self-conscious, but I realize now that there were other things on her mind. At the foot of my street we turned left and passed a half-dozen shops, a record store, a small grocery, an upscale soap store, a travel bureau. She stopped to look at the ticket prices in the window but quickly moved out of the light when I caught up to her. I picked a dark restaurant and we went in. It was Thursday night, late, and we got a good table near the front.

"Are you sure you want to sit here?" she asked.

"Yes," I said. "This is my favourite table."

"Your wife or something's not going to walk by?"

"I don't have a wife."

"You're an exception."

"To what?"

"To all the people who go in that place." She looked at the menu. "What can I have?"

"Anything you want. How about you?"

"What about me?" She was looking at the menu, but she was waiting for the next question.

"Are you married?"

"Not really."

"Does he know what you do?"

"What do you mean, what I do?"

"You know, the sex trade?"

It was a stupid thing to have said. She put down the menu. "I don't work in the sex trade."

"Of course you do. There's nothing wrong with it. You just do."

"So you're saying I'm a whore."

"Good heavens, no."

But she was right. I could feel the alcohol awakening a kind of careless aggression, and I suddenly remembered a foolish quarrel I had had with Emma in Thailand. It was about childbirth, about who had the more profound understanding of the experience, a woman who'd never had a child or a male doctor who had delivered hundreds of babies. Lord! It started during a blood red sunset, too gorgeous to express, and went on until after dark. What I remember is not who said what but rather a glimpse I got of Emma during it—as a sort of foul-tempered little sprite with a vindictive streak.

The memory of that evening is, of course, hopelessly compromised by alcohol, but after she'd moved out, when I waited second by second for her to telephone, when she knew I was waiting, I sometimes had the distinct feeling that it gave her pleasure *not* to call, to look at the telephone by her arm and *not* pick it up. On those few occasions when she did see me—emaciated and wild-eyed, so frightened of her I could barely string a sentence together—I had the feeling that she rather enjoyed her debilitating effect on me. Perhaps she was just a nasty little cunt after all and in her absence I had forgotten that.

Anyway, that evening on the beach in Thailand, she set something off in me. I was indifferent to the subject of childbirth, but something in her manner made me want to squash her in the debate, and I persisted so long that she rose and stormed away. Later, crawling into bed, I was still annoyed, so was she, but in the morning I felt a short, sick sensation when I awoke and remembered the whole foolish affair. What happens to those bad moments? Does sex wipe them away, like that damp cloth on the blackboard? Or do they remain in the heart, one added upon another, a tiff over the dishes here, a disagreement about bullfighting there, an accumulation of nicks and cuts until one morning she looks across the breakfast table and, like Anna Karenina, finds your ears too large or the crunching of your toast repulsive?

A month before she left, we were having lunch in the kitchen. I was hungry and I greedily gobbled up my tuna sandwich.

"I don't want to make you self-conscious," she said, "but you're making a great deal of noise with that sandwich."

She said it politely but in tones that alarmed me at some level. I apologized, but I remember thinking, Hmm, this is new, this has never happened before. One wonders a million things in one's day, so I didn't give it special weight, but I *did* wonder, fleetingly, does she not love me any more? Has she only now noticed this? Or has she only now decided to mention it? Perhaps I was indeed making an intolerable racket, but whatever the reason, something new had happened, I felt sure of that. And even though I didn't think about the incident for months, not until well after she was gone, I have occasionally entertained the private thought that the day things *really* ended with us was not the day of the gently clinking coat hangers in the cupboard but the day with the tuna sandwich. And now, a few years beyond all of it, I'm not at all sure I was wrong.

"I should eat something," I said to Passion. "I'm getting drunk."

It's snobbish to say we had a good time, but we did. A student from my Surrealist course came over and said hello and on the way out introduced his youthful mother. That my pupils might have parents younger than me seemed not so much haunting as vaguely implausible, and as they left the restaurant, watching them go, I again had that flat, unemotional recognition that my life was over.

It was very late when we came back up my street. I don't quite remember the sequence of events after that. I know we had some cognac, after which Passion introduced a joint into the evening. She held it in her fingertips, like a piece of rare chocolate, and leaned her long neck forward to inhale it. Normally I stay away from that stuff, not for moral reasons but because it speeds up my brain to an intolerable level of negative introspection. But, muffled as it was by the blanket of alcohol, the groans and thrashings of my subconscious never made it to the surface.

I must have dozed off. I have a vague memory of the doorbell ringing, a taxi for Passion. I woke up at six o'clock in the morning on the chesterfield with a splitting headache, such a comic-strip hangover that I laughed giddily standing over the toilet bowl. I turned on the tap to help me, but the running water sounded like sneering English soccer fans. I looked in the mirror. My lips were caked with red wine. The flesh seemed swollen under my chin. The evening, which had seemed adventurous, now assumed a kind of frightening sordidness, as if I were en route to something from which I needed saving.

I opened the medicine cabinet, but I couldn't find my codeine tablets, which was odd because I always left them in the same place. I checked on the floor, behind the toilet (bending over gave me the sensation of a large chunk of ice sliding forward inside my head); I even looked, inexplicably, in the bathtub. This was puzzling. I wandered into the kitchen and flipped through the cupboard beside the stove. I came across a near empty bottle of sleeping pills; I must have forgotten about it when I renewed my prescription. I shook a green capsule into my hand and went back to bed. I could hear a noise, a small clinking. It was the empty hangers in my cupboard, clinking together exactly as they had the night Emma left.

It came over me soon enough, the taste of bitter almonds, a sign the pill was seeping into my blood, seeping up into my brain. The headache receded and so did the sense of sin. I took a deeper breath. My body relaxed. The world's dirty teeth loosened on my heart. I had not, after all, been privy to a sudden revolting *aperçu* of myself, as the bloated landlord of some discount store. No, I had simply drunk too much. *Il ne faut pas s'y tromper.* And yet, where a sleeping pill usually puts me out for four or five hours, this time I woke up an hour later, consciousness rising like a shark's fin up, up through the dark water, breaking the surface. Yes, there *was* something wrong, I could feel it.

I lay in bed, my eyes still closed, running over the events of the evening: the phone call, the massage, the dinner, even the off-colour remark about the skin trade. What else? We'd talked about her boyfriend. Her boyfriend, the bank robber. How exotic it had seemed, me out in the world dining with a gangster's girlfriend, a black one at that. A little piece of film noir that had unspooled itself in my head throughout the evening, during which, with each successive glass of wine, I had become more and more the angular leading man. I recalled with a slight shudder the encounter with my Surrealism student and his mother and the private pleasure I'd taken later in how I must seem to them, how surprised they must have been, talking and talking and talking about me afterwards. What an interesting fellow I was! One would have thought starchy, stiff, but there I was, a professor of French literature out on the town with a black woman, easy as can be. Even the waiters knew my name. *Another half-litre, Professor Halloway?* A man of the world.

How sordid it seemed now in this February light, a crow cawing down by the lake, the world so still, as if waiting for something, the sky pearl-coloured, the sun dull like polished silver, creeping through a crack in the venetian blinds. How odd that the sun would pick this very moment to sit at exactly the only place in the sky where it could break through the only break in my venetian blinds. But I was doing it again, delaying, putting off. What was it, what was the *problem?* What was bothering me?

I retrieved my dressing gown from the floor, where it lay like an executed man, and went cautiously into the living room. At first

I noticed nothing wrong. I looked around the room. A candle burnt down to the nub, the wax hardened on the hardwood table. Sloppy but fixable. A smell of stale cigarette smoke. Two wineglasses, one on its side but unbroken. No wine stains on the carpet, no cigarette burns on the tabletop. Nothing permanent. I had just bent over to right the wineglass when I noticed, on the table beside the couch, a clear circular spot the size of the bottom of a glass. A light film of dust covered the rest of the table. My house, largely because of the fireplace, was very dusty; it gummed up my computer mouse, my CD player, watered the eyes of allergic guests. Except for this round space. Because I was hungover, a kind of glue coated my thoughts and stuck them shapelessly together. For that reason it took me some minutes to understand what was going on. There had been something on that table, something with a round base. But what? I couldn't remember, the way that sometimes, when pressed, you can't remember your phone number or where you left your car. I stared at the table and then the whole sickening picture came into focus. A frosted glass statue of the Madonna, a foot tall and very pricey, was gone. I'd inherited it from my mother; it was the only thing of hers I'd kept. I looked on the floor beside the sofa, under it. And then I noticed the other things. A cigarette lighter, my gold pocket watch (which Emma had returned), a Mexican ashtray, all missing. A pewter flask from the sideboard, a delicate bracelet from a long-departed sleepover, all of it gone. I saw clearly now the image of Passion getting out of the taxi with that over-large handbag. It was black velveteen, with red markings like lightning on the side.

Then I remembered the clank I'd heard down the hall, the sound I couldn't identify. Of course: it was the medicine cabinet opening, the glass door banging against its hinges. The bitch. She'd even swiped my codeine tablets.

CHAPTER 9

Months passed and with them the winter. Buds popped on the trees, the air turned soft and you could smell the wet earth. I went to a conference in Toulouse, my old stomping ground. The town was almost unrecognizable to me. I looked for old cafés and they were gone. I tried to look up my old Spanish roommate, but I couldn't even find the street I remembered he lived on. Entire neighbourhoods seemed switched about.

I gave a paper on a new poem, allegedly by Rimbaud, which had recently turned up in a forgotten literary journal; there had been only one or two issues before it went under. After only one reading I was convinced it was a hoax; there was a kind of hothouse feel to it, the images too jammed together to suggest the effortless imagination of this young truant from the north country. In fact, on my second evening in Toulouse, I was having a drink after dinner when it came to me that there was something oddly familiar, not in the language but in the rhythm of the poem's final rhyming couplet. I'd heard it somewhere before—and not in Rimbaud either. I stayed up much of the night flipping through Baudelaire, through all sorts of poets, anyone who might have had an influence on Rimbaud. By three that morning I came to the conclusion that Paul Verlaine, his lover, had written the poem as a parody and submitted it under his friend's name. It was just the kind of thing those two might well have got up to one drunken afternoon.

I presented the paper the following day. It was greeted apathetically, as if I were a sort of spoilsport, except by Serrault, who was there to give a paper on "The Clown as Social Transgressor." He agreed with me. Besides, he said, it was a second-rate poem anyway.

It was shortly after my return that I experienced a series of irritating bits of bad luck. It was not destiny fulfilling itself, nothing like that. Rather, it seemed like stubbing your toe two or three times on the same bedpost. Infuriating. I lost my Proust pencil, for example (for underlining the hardback version). Then I lost my wallet. Even after I'd cancelled my credit cards, I couldn't seem to stop looking for it. In my shorts, in the back pocket of my blue suit, even in my shirts, as if you could possibly miss a falafel-sized wallet in the breast pocket of a shirt! I searched the clothes I'd worn the day before, the month before, I sniffed around my house, I looked in the African flower

vase three, four, five times. It just went on and on, this crazy looking, as if I were some kind of mute animal that had lost its cub on the
Serengeti. I looked and looked and looked, and I always ended up in
a rage. I hurled the entire contents of my clothing cabinet onto the
floor; sweaters, socks, towels, scarves I hadn't seen in years, everything right there onto the floor. Including a pair of jeans that Emma
had left behind. My, she had such a small waist. I laid the jeans out
on my bed and for a second I stood there amidst the mess and the
linen and the bundles of clothes and looked down at this set of jeans
lying on the bed as if her body, her soul, had only seconds before
soared from them. I lay down very carefully and I put my face in the
crotch of the jeans. But they had been in the cupboard too long. She
was gone.

I searched in my car, under the seat, under the dash. I banged my
head on the mirror. To calm myself I sat very still and took a number of deep breaths. I could feel the magma changing colour in the
centre of my head and I made a decision to let the wallet go, to go
inside that very second and initiate the next tedious set of phone
calls. I opened the car door and a passing Jeep, which had come up
soundlessly during my reverie, took the door off at the hinges. The
car screamed as if its arm had been torn away.

A half-hour later, after some belligerent give-and-take with a
very unattractive woman—the driver of the car—I called a tow
truck company, and twenty minutes after that a dirty-fingernailed,
tabloid-reading thug pulled up in a half-ton with a crane on the back.
He wanted to be paid in advance. I didn't have a credit card, so I had

to take a taxi to the fucking bank while he waited in the driveway with his meter on. His words, not mine.

I was making the hurried withdrawal, the cab still waiting, when the teller, a dark-eyed Pakistani woman, interrupted her calculations with an upward glance and a short, "Oh!" I had the unaccountable feeling that I should brace myself.

"Your friend Emma?" she said, her voice rising in a singsong.

I felt the blood leave my face. "I haven't seen Emma for ages," I replied coldly.

"Come *on*," she said, and gave me an impertinent wink as if I were a well-known scoundrel contriving to pull a fast one.

"No," I said quite deliberately, trying to control my voice, trying to control the impulse to punch her in the face, "I haven't." But the question—and my attempt, my need, to convince this *cunt* of my insouciance—left me quite breathless. I was sure she could hear it and I had the impression that my face was changing colour, a beacon to communicate to the world that I had been whipped raw by a young woman and that even the mention of her name still made me yelp with discomfort.

"Then you don't know she's pregnant?"

"How wonderful," I said, and as the words came from my mouth I heard myself thinking, Good, I sound convincing, a lover of babies and forgiver of betrayals. And as for you, I thought, looking at the teller, at her bovine brown eyes, her beefy hips, *you* I'll fix later. It enraged me that a teller had presumed to accost me on such a personal matter. Surely she had been seeking to wound me, to embarrass me.

"I suppose you'll be sending your congratulations," she said.

"I beg your pardon?"

"Your congratulations to Emma for her pregnancy?"

I had the sensation of time slowing down as I've heard it does for a great athlete. A kind of murderous calm took hold of me. There was no hurry now.

"What I *can* tell you," I said with deliberate slowness, "is that I don't want to discuss my personal life with a teller when I come to do a piece of simple banking."

She looked at me as if I'd just laid an exotically veined dildo on the counter alongside my bank book. Inexplicable as it may sound, I felt terrific, as if I had just struck a blow against an oppressor or scored a goal in the last second of a hockey match. They were child-like sensations of delight and surging pleasure. I was back in the taxi and ten blocks away before I understood what it was that had so pleased me. It was *relief.* For the first time since Emma left me, I had given public utterance to my rage for the pain that had been visited upon me. For the fact that she had never called or written or come to see me. That I could have been swinging from a rope in my house, my throat slashed, my shirt stiff with coagulated blood, and she had never so much as stopped by to see if I was alive. And that I should hear such a thing—she was having a baby!– from a teller. How curious an end stories and people and love affairs come to.

From a teller.

I came home, paid off the tow truck driver, fetched a bottle of wine, some cheese and a few cigarettes, and took them out on the porch for a bit of a think. I was waiting for the shock, I suppose, from the news of Emma's pregnancy, the bang that comes from a sniper's rifle a moment after you've seen the puff of smoke. But it didn't come, and I assumed it meant I'd already given up on her.

It was rather interesting out there, actually, plopped in my wicker chair, feet on the balcony, watching the goings-on in the street: the neighbours coming in and out of their houses, cars parking, cars pulling away, dogs running down the street, children passing by. Like watching one of those educational movies of a plant growing. I found myself thinking about all sorts of things.

Near eight I went down to the corner for a drink. I felt like being in the presence of human bodies, but I didn't like the company there; something rather irritated me about the place, about the foolish opinions that spilled over into my range of hearing. Silly people with silly ideas. I drifted along Bloor Street, stopping here and there, never quite satisfied, when suddenly I threw up my arm and flagged down a cab. I had a hunch there was something downtown for me.

I got out on College Street and started walking west. Crossed that little street by the bank machine. Without knowing why, I went into an upstairs blues club. I hadn't been there for years. The girl on the door let me in for free, a sign, I assumed, that I was meant to be there. I sat at a corner table. A band was playing. The air was thick with blue cigarette smoke and happy chat. At the table next to mine a young man, reminiscent of someone I had known in university, held forth, his companions, both boys and girls, leaning forward with a look of anticipatory pleasure on their young faces. How generous they seemed, giving over the floor to him; how unbegrudging, how uncompetitive, their open-lipped smiles, the girls tapping their cigarettes on the side of the ashtray and exchanging elated looks. I had the impression of treading water in a tank full of beautiful fish, red and gold and blue and silver. Such youth and beauty and energy, talking of love and boyfriends and girlfriends. Does anyone ever think of anything else? I wondered. *Is* there anything else?

I looked around at the beautiful children and their bright summer clothes and realized abruptly that I didn't belong in this part of town any more. This was, as Dupré might intone, the domain of the becoming.

Still, I remembered. The soaring, the sailing upwards, like the boy at the spellbound next table.

I yawned abruptly. It was time to move on. But where to? Where was I supposed to go? The wind tugged at me. I went down into the subway. When I got to the southbound platform I noticed there was no one about except for a young woman only yards away. She was standing near the tracks, looking down, lost in reverie. About a boy, I assumed. Or maybe a girl. They were everywhere that spring night, those girls that make you slightly pale. She had dark, short hair, jeans and leather moccasins, and wore a silver necklace so delicate you could barely see it. I sat down on the bench and stared at her. Stared and stared. I think she knew I was staring and I expected her to move off, but she didn't.

The train arrived. I heard it rumble at the far end of the tunnel, saw its bright central light snap into being; I got on board and sat where I could watch her. I imagined introducing myself. What would I say? I would say, Have you read Maupassant? *Pas du tout?* Why, there's a story about a young girl just like you and a man on the train, just like me, who watches her. Watches her and watches her and . . . Well, I hope you'll forgive this impertinence, but I'd like you to read it. Read it and think of me. And then I would give her my card: *Professor Halloway, Ph.D. (Chicago)*. I'd write my home phone number on the back. Dear me, what good joke could I make? Something about Baudelaire. Verlaine maybe. Perhaps even that bit about Jarry walking the lobster on a leash; that had never really had its proper day. And then, with slightly bashful goodbyes, we would separate, there on the subway platform. How smart I would be not to presume. Weeks would go by; I'd forget about her almost entirely. And then one evening, when the fall air blows under the back door and I have to lay down a rolled-up towel to keep the draft from blowing under the crack, on such a night as that, the children dressed as hobgoblins ringing my doorbell, on such a night as that she would call . . .

But I smelt of alcohol and I didn't want her to think I was *that* kind of person. She looked up and tilted her head, just so, as if she were reading a slightly puzzling billboard across the tracks, or perhaps so I could see even more clearly how beautiful she was, her pointed chin, her wide forehead. I looked for a flaw, but the more I stared the more beautiful she became, until I felt quite ill. I imagined kissing her exquisite neck. I closed my eyes and imagined touching my lips to her skin, right there, below her ear.

A man in a brown suit and a wig got on the train. Standing discreetly to the side, he looked about, here, there, like a mouse in a dark room, until he caught sight of her, and then he too stared at her, the both of us. I had the impression that, coming in, he had seen her and found a place where, like me, he could observe with impunity. But each second I looked at her grew more painful; it said to me, you'll never have her, never be with her, that part of your life is over. And suddenly I could hardly wait for her to leave the train.

She got out at Union Station. Looking this way and then that, she moved down the platform. The train started up. I tried to force myself not to look at her as we passed because I knew I'd be looking for her to be looking back into the train and she wouldn't be, a clear sign that she hadn't even noticed me. But as we drew abreast I had to look. What if she *had* been looking back? What if that was the point of the evening?

The train rattled on through into the tunnel.

It was half past eleven when I came up my street. In the park a clutch of teenagers sat on the knoll smoking cigarettes. The wind gently stirred the branches overhead; you could hear them whisper, *swish, swish, swish*. Suddenly I was very tired, my head ached, my eyes felt as if tiny grains of sand were rubbing against the insides of my eyelids.

I don't remember going to bed. Sometime near morning I had a dream about Emma. And such a dream! I'd had it before. Let me explain, please. I had *two* Emmas in my life. One was the Emma who had left me a good while ago and in the interim had become an anecdote. She was, and here I'm being ingenuous, a wound I believed to be long since healed. But then there was *another* Emma, the one who dwelt in my heart. This was the Emma I had slept beside for nearly three years. Sometimes in the middle of the night I would slip my hand under her arm and then return my fingers, now smelling of her, to their resting place between my face and the pillow. Sometimes, only half awake, she raised her thin arm, just an inch or two, to help me. When I thought about *that* Emma, it still filled me with hollowing grief, as if a creature were moving around my chest seeking a point of exit.

Anyway. My dream. I dreamt that we were in a country house, her friends there; young, affluent couples, glib young men; Emma and I friendly and talkative (Emma the anecdote); everything going swimmingly; no one aware, it seemed, of the incongruity of us—Emma and I—not being together any more, of her being with *someone else*. Not even I. She had crossed her legs, I remember, and was picking distractedly at the side of her loafer, but her restlessness, her shifting attention, set me off. Suddenly, sickeningly, she became the *second* Emma. And the simple, ungraspable fact of her absence woke me from a dead sleep with the conviction, the *certainty*, that someone had just shouted something in my ear and then vanished from the room.

"Emma?" I whispered, looking around in the dark.

I could feel the sensation of her presence moving away like footsteps down a hospital hallway in the middle of the night. It was of such a bewildering immediacy, it seemed that she had just left the room, that the air still moved where she had passed.

It was nearly noon when I awoke, but I was fearsomely hungover. I planned my day. I would get up and brush my teeth and have a cup of coffee and put on my shorts and sweatshirt and go for a run up in my old neighbourhood. I'd run and run, and by the time I got back, maybe forty-five minutes later, I could start the day.

But I didn't do that.

Instead, I got up and brushed my teeth and put on a pair of pants, an old work shirt and a pair of loafers. I didn't bother with socks. I walked up to Dupont and headed east, and just the notion that I didn't have to jog, that I wouldn't have to face the day-long, roller-coaster swings of a hangover made me feel almost healthy. By the time I burst through the doors I was in a fine mood.

"Never underestimate the joys of jogging to the liquor store," I announced to the bewildered patrons.

I returned a moment later to the cashier with a Mondavi Reserve, the doctor having advised me that it is better to drink expensive wines than cheap ones. Then I hesitated. Surely, by buying only one bottle, I was asking for trouble. If you have *one* bottle, you're constantly aware of running out, of being halfway there, two-thirds the way there, and so on right down to the last glass. It's not a melodramatic craving for liquor; rather, it's the nuisance of having to go back to the liquor store. Whereas if you buy two, you always have more than you need. You can have another glass or not without having to deal with the implications of where that leaves things, the imminent "Damn, I'm running low."

I bought four bottles and then stopped off at the Hong Kong variety store and bought a package of cigarettes. Coming down the street, bottles clanking like a ship's bell, I ran across my Australian neighbour. That clipped, lughead accent. He lived in a mildly depressing house. I can't say exactly why it was depressing, perhaps the small windows or the gloomy porch, but a sense of ennui fell over me whenever I passed by. Today he was out on the front lawn plonking in the garden. He was a gutty, red-faced fellow who felt a compulsion to accompany even the simplest greeting with a put-down of some kind. He did this, I think, so that you took him seriously. You may be a professor of literature, *mate*, but I'm up to your game any day of the week. Not just up to it either, but *on to it* as well, because there was, in his sly questionings about my life, the implication that I was pulling a scam that he alone was sophisticated enough to perceive. That he might ruffle feelings or even hurt them in his quest to be taken seriously apparently never occurred to him.

For the past few months I'd had a feeling that we were moving into dark waters and had tried to duck him. But today, pulling weeds from his flower bed, he must have heard me coming, because he looked up with a cunning smile. For some reason I veered straight at him, stepping off the sidewalk and crossing the street. *Clank, clank,* went my little black friends.

"Getting an early start?'" he said.

"Never mind that, sissy boy. Just get back to your weeds."

He stepped back, understandably astonished. It was a bewildering non sequitur delivered with such venom that even his dog, working alongside him, looked up. He issued an explosive laugh. I could see I'd alarmed him, and in my worsening mood I experienced a kind of epiphany. Now that I had abused him, however mildly, he would suddenly, without knowing why, find himself admiring me; people like him develop a sort of mutt-like affection for the very people who give them a good smack on the beak with the evening paper. But while he may have cried out for it, the discomfort shooting across his features somewhat curdled my pleasure. I had thought it would be more fun than this. So, having stuck it in, I now hurried to take it out.

"Have you ever had one of those days when you just give up?" I asked. From my tone of eager curiosity it sounded as if I put a very high premium indeed on his response.

He nodded cautiously.

"I'm having one of those days," I went on, this delivered with what appeared to be candour and chatty vulnerability.

"I thought you had a bit of a slag on," he said.

Ugh. A professional Aussie. *Rien de plus emmerdant.* Honestly, it made me want to have another go at him. Furthermore, I couldn't help noticing a glob of dried egg on his chin. He'd neglected to wipe his face after breakfast. A knob's knob. Still, I had a feeling that from now on our chit-chats would take a more formal tone. A great thing, formality. What those pampered little prickweeds in the sixties never understood—spoilt, parasitic bottom-lickers that they were—was that in many cases, and certainly when it comes to people expressing their *real* feelings, repression is a good thing.

Arriving home, I discovered that I was no longer in so grand a hurry to throw off my hangover. Just the proximity of the four bottles, the fact of their absolute availability, comforted me. I opened the California to let it breathe. I found an ashtray, opened the cigarettes, laid them on the counter, tidied up the kitchen, put the dishes in the dishwasher, got the place shipshape so that in the eventuality of another hangover I would at least find myself in a tidy madhouse. Speaking of which, I was on my way into the bathroom to check on my supply of sleeping pills when the telephone rang. I picked up the receiver, but there was no one there; the line hung open and with a click the hum resumed. Idiotically, I wondered if it was Emma Carpenter. I could see her holding the phone, her sharp nose, her dry lips. I could see her standing motionless in an empty house with the phone in her hand, and with that image I had a rather frightening sensation that there was something moving toward me, like a shadow in the water, slowly and surely closing off the yards; that all I had to do was wait, to stay put, and it would reveal itself.

But while I pondered this thing that moved slowly toward me, it suddenly occurred to me that it might have been Passion who phoned. Passion and her bank robber boyfriend calling to see if I was home, setting up my house for another hit. I went down to the basement and got my gun from behind the furnace. I cleaned off the cobwebs with a rag, brought it back upstairs and rested it on the foyer table.

Then I started drinking. My oh my, where didn't I go that afternoon? As the day wore on I found myself on foreign shores. Let me stop for a moment. I haven't been entirely candid about my mother, have I? Perhaps I should be now. The truth is that she wasn't a cold woman who barely touched me, not in the beginning anyway. I've told that story so often I've come to believe it myself. The truth is, she adored me. And I adored her back. When I was little I used to believe that the world was full of brown paper bags and useless things, and I thought she did too. I believed that she saw everything, knew everything and loved *everything* about me.

But sometime in my early teenage years she began to turn on me. I could never quite fathom why (I suspect now it was drink and prescription pills), but she became *untrustworthy*, a person to hide things from. Once, when I was fourteen, I came home from school at noon (it was a half day) and found her in my room, rooting through a box of letters, adolescent love letters collected like swimming badges. I could hear her talking to herself, raging and raging and raging. I haven't a clue what she was looking for—proof, perhaps, but of what I don't know. There were other incidents: inexplicable explosions of wrath, the evening she ripped down the shower curtain when I was getting ready to go to a party, her throwing a friend out of the house for looking at her breasts. For a whole summer she ceased to speak to me. She passed me silently in the kitchen, the hallway, the front porch, the living room. I ate my dinner in silence; I went upstairs straight after. She never came up. But I was stronger than her, and I got used to her not loving me any more. I grew skin like cement; I became uncrackable. I shall die before I speak first, I thought, I shall die. And then one evening I heard a thump in the living room. I opened my door silently and went downstairs, and she lay on the floor, those blue eyes still open. And how sad I was. How terribly sad that we didn't get a chance to make up. Because I had always thought we would, had always known she would knock on my door one evening and we'd be friends again. We were *so* fine once, she and I, when I was little, the two of us having a picnic by the side of a lake in Algonquin Park. Such a warm summer day, and I sat on a blanket and the grass waved, the leaves in the trees shushed and shushed, and in that sound I believed they were saying to me, *You will be happy, you will be happy.*

The afternoon wore on. The yellow cat, who now dwelled full-time on my porch, leapt up and settled in my lap. Over the past few months I'd grown rather attached to him. I rubbed him behind the ears where he liked it specially; he purred and moaned and stretched his limbs, his fierce claws extending, finally rolling over in my lap and peering up so that I might rub his tummy. A breeze came up and seemed to blow away the clouds; they hung in wisps as though torn and scattered by the wind.

Surrounded by the shrieks of birds and children, I had the sensation of being swept away on a magic carpet. I turned my head this way and that, and the carpet took me through the city. I saw fantastic sights. I made unusual connections.

I fell asleep.

CHAPTER 10

I awoke at sunset with a foul mouth and a seasick stomach. The last sunlight of the day gleamed off a neighbour's steeple. I smiled into the bathroom mirror. It was a sly smile that insinuated I *knew* something, that we would all know it soon enough. Be patient, it whispered, you'll see.

I left my house in search of a restaurant with white tablecloths and kindly waiters. It seemed such a comforting image, so fresh and clean, that it seemed as if *I* would feel fresh and clean if only I could find it. The sky changed dramatically. Reddish gold clouds hurried in different directions, as if fleeing. One had the impression, walking down my street that early evening, of going through a narrow passageway, the walls of which were smeared with dabs of brightly coloured paint. From the faces coming up the sidewalk—they moved on invisible wheels—I could see I was pursuing an unsteady course. They exchanged quick glances and lowered their heads as if my eyes were fish hooks that might catch them under the chin. Once I looked over my shoulder and saw two white faces at the end of long necks, like daffodils in a field, staring after me. For a fleeting second I thought I recognized them. I may have.

The day rushed to crowd in everything it could before darkness. The clouds had flattened out and lay in pink banks, interspersed here and there with dark blue daubs. A grey tint gathered on lawns, in bushes, in laneways, and with a puff of fragrant breath the day expired. I careened onto Bloor Street, thick now with evening strollers. It was a Friday night and with the alarm of someone who has just remembered leaving a boiling pot of water on the stove, it hit me that there might not be a table for me at the restaurant. Or worse, that it might be the *wrong* table, a table to the side of things, to the side of life. How tedious, how heartbreaking it would be to turn around and go home. Sad Odysseus! For no other restaurant in the world would do. I rushed forward.

"Professor Halloway?"

I heard it from somewhere behind me. It was a woman's voice, but it registered on my nervous system like an intrusion, as if a stranger had grabbed me aggressively by the shoulder and swung me around. Standing in front of me was a young woman with black bangs.

"It's Katrina," she said. "From your French class." I recognized her, but it mustn't have registered on my features because she rushed on with, "I gave the seminar on Boileau. *L'art poétique.* You've probably forgotten."

"No. Not at all," I said. "Quite the opposite."

"What are you doing in this neighbourhood?" she asked.

"I live here," I said. "Not *here* here. But nearby."

She hiccuped. "Good heavens," she said, covering her mouth with a small hand, her eyes wide with surprise, "ex*cuse* me," and there was something in the gesture that made me want to reach out and touch her face. But like the rumbling of a tin sheet in an amateur theatrical, I could hear a warning not to. I gave a deep sigh. The street lights came on with an audible click.

She said something in French.

"What?" I said.

"Is my accent that bad? It's from Boileau. You know, that part where he says that the words that come to you first are usually the right words. It's, like, the most famous part."

I took a long, unsteady look at her. "Katrina, you have the most beautiful skin. I hope that doesn't embarrass you."

But even as these words issued from my lips I could see her face darken, distort, and for a second I forgot whom I was talking to.

"Professor Halloway, you've had a *long* day," she said, and with the sound of her voice she came back into focus. She really *was* beautiful.

"I'm rather drunk, it's true, Katrina," I said.

"Well, that's all right," she said, "everyone gets drunk occasionally."

"Do they?"

"So I've heard."

I had entertained a faint, wild hope that she might join me, come along for this peculiar evening, but her last sentence was like a polite disengaging.

"Even you?" I asked.

"I've got no head for it. One drink and I'm gone. Poof. You wouldn't want to be around for that."

*Yes, I would. I'd like very much to be around for that.*

"What do you do?" I asked.

"I'm still in school."

"No, I mean when you're drunk."

"Oh, stuff."

"What sort of stuff?"

I wanted her to say . . . well, it's obvious, isn't it? It must have been obvious to her too, because she added quickly, looking away, like a caboose separating from the main body of the train, "Fall asleep usually."

There. Now it was clear. Surely you don't need to hear more, I thought. In fact—and *écoute bien, toi*—if you leave now, you're safe. No morning horrors. No jerking upright in bed as the ruins of the evening come back to you. In a word, nothing to be ashamed of.

"I must go," I said.

But I didn't. Not immediately, anyway. It's in those moments that your life is decided, or so it seemed at that very second. I put out my hand and very gently touched the side of her face. "I've wanted to do that for ages."

She went very still.

"Good night, Katrina," I said.

And she said, "Good night, Professor Halloway."

I didn't turn around, not once, not all the way to the restaurant, but the encounter had illuminated me, and I burst into the crowded dining room and settled at a table near the centre, just on the aisle, facing the window. The dream table. Draped in white, as if it had been waiting for me and me alone, it sat at the very centre of all things. I felt an almost romantic gratitude to the waiter, who offered me a drink, the kind a cold man might experience who is allowed to come indoors to warm up. In such circumstances a waiter assumes the stature of an authority figure, a man whose approval one is keen to cultivate. How strangely important waiters are! I felt such extraordinary warmth and affection for all of them, for their bustle and high spirits; how smooth they were, in white shirts and black slacks, gliding among the tables. One of them, an elegant blond boy, slim and lean, stopped to shake my hand. "Nice to see you again, Professor, " to which I replied, "Lovely to be back." Lord. The rapture, the transport, of finding the right restaurant. I could actually feel a sensation of pleasure rippling my blood. And in a moment a carafe of deep red wine, lovely in the candlelight, appeared in front of me as the waiter cleared off the setting opposite me. He poured me a glass and then with a small flourish set down the carafe.

"When you're ready, Professor," he said.

Really, I was almost too happy. I must *do* something for these fellows, I thought, something to express my ineffable gratitude. Perhaps I'll bring in one of my books, perhaps the one on Baudelaire's early criticism, and give it, no, *dedicate* it to these waiters. Sign it. Yes, that's what I'll do. What a gorgeous idea. What pleasure that will give to all. Odd not to have thought of it before.

"Pro*fessor* Halloway." A man's voice this time, a few tables over, a bearded man and his wife, who beamed identical grins at me.

"Ah yes," I said, not having a clue who they were but granting them nevertheless a somewhat papal wave.

The waiter returned. "You're quite a celebrity, Professor Halloway. Why, just a few moments ago a girl over there asked me if I knew you. I think she's one of your students."

I wondered if Katrina had followed me in. I looked over. "Where is she?"

"She's gone now."

"Hmm." I stroked my chin thoughtfully. "Pity. But yes, yes indeed, I *am* having quite the evening."

"Would you like to order now?" he asked.

In the flush of such stimulation my appetite had vanished. In fact, the very idea of eating seemed a tad depressing, as if (bear with me) in the image of my taking a meal, hands clicking busily with knife and fork over a dish of *Foie de Veau à l'ancienne*, I could also make out in the background an empty, rather desolate dining hall, like one might find in a restored castle, but empty, you see, no one there, just the lord of the mansion dining by himself at the end of day . . . Ah, that was it. It was the *end of day* part I didn't like, as a teenager is inexpressibly depressed by the sounds of certain television shows on a Sunday night.

"I can give you a few more minutes."

"That would be lovely."

"Another carafe?"

"In a few minutes."

He moved away. The bearded man at the nearby table said something to his escort and came over. I partially stood, but he waved me down.

"I saw you on the educational channel," he said. "I thought you were terrific. I particularly enjoyed that remark about Lautréamont . . ."

Seeing a mist of well-meaning confusion in my eyes (a look I had deliberately planted there because I knew exactly and precisely what he was referring to but wanted, for the purposes of my own insatiable vanity, to hear it restated, not to mention the planting in his bushy head of the notion that I dropped these *bons mots* here and there like a maiden dropping flower petals, whereas I had, in fact, rehearsed that very remark over and over, a dozen times, on the way to the studio, to the degree where I noticed a fellow subway passenger staring as if I were a madman talking to himself), he obliged me by saying, with relish, as if he had a tasty bit of roast beef in his mouth, "You said that Lautréamont was The Monkees of the Symbolist movement. I can't stop repeating it."

I chuckled appreciatively, as if to suggest no, I didn't recall the remark, per se, but its very outrageousness was something that, with a certain amount of resignation, I had come to expect from myself after all these years. How charming was my self-effacement.

"Anyway," he said, extending his hand, which I shook, "you were like a *wreck*ing ball."

"That's a compliment, I gather."

"Indeed it is."

His wife waved shyly. The second carafe arrived at the table. He bowed ever so slightly and withdrew.

I pondered this "Monkees of the Symbolist movement" remark for a bit, and gradually, like cocaine, its effulgence wore off. In effect, it did not inspire quite the transcending echo of *arma virumque cano*. But it did set off some rather odd thoughts about Arthur Rimbaud. For a split second I believed I *had* him, this ungraspable young genius who had abandoned poetry at nineteen. I believed I saw with absolute clarity not the meaning of his work— he was too good for that—but rather how his brain worked, the poetic process by which he arrived at the imagery of his final *Illuminations*. I understood them not as a coherent message hiding in a coded language, a code that God-hungry undergraduates or tenured duffers claimed occasionally to crack, but rather as a series of extraordinary associations *for and of themselves*. It was a thought that came to me through the side door, so to speak, a thought I *caught* myself having rather than one I had set out to have and wrestled into lifelessness, like the marlin ripped from the ocean whose colour dies within seconds of its flesh pounding the gunnel of the boat.

I called over the waiter and asked for pen and paper, which he supplied, and I began to write in a large, confident hand. At which point the shriek of a chair leg on the tile floor drew my attention to the window, where I saw Katrina, I'm sure, walk by on the street. Sensation compounded sensation, but I continued to write, my attention focused like a laser beam on the thought processes—like a fast-motion view of a pearl forming in the shell of an oyster—of this lanky boy from the northern provinces. For six pages I wrote clearly and calmly before putting down the pen.

She was long gone by then, Katrina, and I wondered why I had not risen from my seat and chased out into the street after her. Perhaps because we had parted on such a good note that to see her again the same evening, even drunker now than before, might abrogate a possibility down the road. Yes, possibly that was it. But somehow I didn't feel the satisfaction with that answer that you get when you've truly solved a problem. No, it was something else, something more elemental perhaps: the possibility that sex might not be all I had heretofore believed it to be; that it might be instead a sort of subway stop on the way to somewhere else. What a curious thought, that sex, this thing which had always struck me as the heart of the matter, might be only a way of clearing your head, rather like clearing a table, so that you could get down to the *real* business of life. But what was that? Well, one's work, of course. One's *real* work. I sighed abruptly. It had been unnecessary, I reasoned further, for me to pursue a course of action (running after Katrina and, in a perfect world, going to bed with her) because I was already doing (working) what I would invariably return to in the cool-headed aftermath. Which led me to an equally unfamiliar conclusion: that my choice to teach, and to teach French literature in particular, had not been as casual, as arbitrary, as I'd thought, the response to a teenage jilting, but rather an act of self- preservation, an instinctive nudging toward—get this—happiness. The notion that for years and years I had actually been working *toward* my happiness as opposed to *against* it struck me as a revelation of biblical proportion.

I looked around the restaurant.

Suddenly I realized I was starving. There was a nervous ache in my stomach, which hinted at a piece of shuddering machinery. I swept my gaze down the menu and with a feeling of fiscal impunity ordered the lamb chops.

"They take about twenty minutes."

"Splendid," I said. The waiter refilled my glass with a flourish.

The noise in the restaurant increased. From over near the bar, behind which a young man prepared an after-dinner tray of coffees, I heard a flamenco guitar, whose hesitant introductory notes announced themselves and then appeared to stand in the foyer, waiting to be invited the rest of the way into the room. I listened carefully. I knew that piece of music, knew where it was going next. The guitarist responded with a flourish and then another. A pair of girls beside me, one pregnant, were talking about a trip to Aruba, the nuisance of lining up at the airport three hours before the flight. I was eavesdropping on them when the name came to me: *Concierto de Aranjuez*, the first symphony, I recalled, to be composed for the acoustic guitar. But it had been used in so many westerns that one could not hear it without also seeing the cliché of a cowboy walking down the centre of a windswept Mexican street. And yet it was a rather compelling image, this man with the cigarillo. Stirring almost, in a way you would never want to admit.

I took a sudden, involuntary deep breath, as if my body had commanded it. How like the days of my childhood today had been. How *symphonic*. There was no other word for it. And my goodness, what a long day. Well, hardly a day, for time seemed attenuated, like soft toffee pulled slowly over two or three days, the variegated incidents stuck like stones, some precious, some vulgar, here and there. The day, it seemed now, had started almost a year before. The day of the clinking hangers.

I laughed softly and stirred in my chair. The pregnant woman looked over, then went on talking. "I told him to wait for the phone call, but he said he's coming on the eighteenth anyway. I said, Daddy, the baby might not *be* here yet . . ." My, she talked a lot. How difficult for her husband, all that chatter, and now the two of them trapped in the kitchen for two years, watching an infant wave and gurgle and poop and . . . I suppose, though, that even if Emma came back now, it'd be impossible. A teller in a bank. Who could have imagined that would be the last of things? Hmm. The last of things. There was a whole list of things that you did for the last time with someone. The last time I slept with her, yes, I remembered that; thrashing away at her poor young body because I couldn't come. Those pills. Prozac . . . no, not Prozac, its cousin. Anyway, doesn't matter. Too bad, though, to end that way. Sort of anticlimactic. There was a last dinner, a last good night, a last hug in the middle of the night, the last time she

brushed her teeth over my sink, that last time she dried her hair in
the bathroom. No one knew it. As one doesn't. As one won't when
at the end of one's life there will be a last time to make love, a last
time to close a novel and lay it on the floor beside the bed, a last
time to pull the curtains, a last movie. A last time to see one's
mother. A last morning. And yet one can't complain. You're only
entitled to so much life. No, if you were to say to me, tomorrow is
your last, I think I might think, I can't complain, not really. I've
had a bit of love, a bit of fame, a bit of sex. A bit of this and that
and then goodbye. But what happens to one's things? The books,
for example. There's a last time for each of those books too; no
farewell, just a final glance at their pages. A last time for Rimbaud,
for Balzac, for Zola, for Lautréamont even. The Monkees of the
Symbolist movement. How little that matters now. How little it ever
mattered. But you have always known that; have always known
that somehow none of *that* mattered. Love mattered. Or was it
love? No, probably not. For when Emma left I wanted her dead.
How loving was that? (Here I smiled.) No, not murdered, not
that. But a sad accident perhaps, where afterwards I might doff my
hat, my eyes watering, and say, yes, how dreadful, such a fine
young woman. Me at her funeral beside her father, shrunk with
grief, her mother fussing about the reception, the food. "I want
everyone gone by six," she'd say. "After that they can bloody well
mix their own drinks."

The *Aranjuez* more insistent now. I looked around the room.
The pace of things had picked up; the talk was louder; the silverware

clanked more aggressively; the waiters moved faster. Like the concerto, the evening felt as if it were moving toward something. But what? I wondered. What?

Things began to rankle, the pregnant woman still talking. God, will she never shut up? I thought pregnant women were holy women, not such screeching chatterboxes. How *does* her husband put up with it?

"Darius?"

*Is it you, my little princess? Come to save me from the fires of hell? I fear you've come too late.*

"Darius Halloway?"

An older woman, elegantly dressed, thick in the waist, stood before my table. Her hair grey now, once frizzy, was pulled tightly into a bun at the back of her neck. High cheekbones supported a weary, smiling face.

"It's Raissa," she said.

"Raissa?"

"Raissa Shestatsky."

From a swirl of clothes and tired features my beautiful young philosophy student stepped suddenly forward, like a child who has been hiding under the covers jumps up to surprise her parents.

"My God," I whispered.

"Of all the days I had to run into you, it would have to be today when I'm looking like hell warmed over."

Yes, I recognized her voice now. But who was the white-haired man behind her?

"You look lovely," I said. I opened my mouth, but nothing more came out. I tried again. "I haven't seen you in thirty years."

"If a day. Yes, I was sitting over there. I didn't want to disturb you. You're the only man I've ever known who can do nothing and still appear busy."

"But it's so lovely to see you again. Can you sit down?"

"No, we're on our way out. I see you on television sometimes. I don't know what the hell you're saying, but it sounds interesting. I ended up teaching too. High school."

"Do you still read Heidegger?"

"No, I outgrew all that."

"But Raissa, you look so lovely. Can't you stay a moment?"

She turned and said something to her friend, the white-haired man, who stepped forward.

"This is my husband, Richard."

A pleasant-faced man with a slight accent introduced himself.

"He's going to get the car," she said.

"But sit down, sit down."

"I saw one of your books in the store, oh, ages ago, and I thought to myself, the son of a gun did it."

"Which one?"

She looked at me with some confusion.

"I mean, there are more than one."

"Oh," she said, "I don't know."

I looked at her again. I wanted to weep. "Raissa."

"Darius," she said with some humour.

"You won't believe this, but I was thinking about you only a few days ago. I was trying to think of the last time we saw each other," I said.

"That's easy," she said briskly. "It was after you came back from France. We had coffee together."

"I thought there was another time. After that."

"No, we never saw each other again."

"It's odd in so small a city, where I run into everyone," I said.

"I don't live down here. I live in the suburbs."

"But you don't come down here? *Ever?*" I asked in a strangely imploring tone.

"No, never. Besides, it was clear you didn't love me any more."

"Raissa."

"When we had coffee together, I could see you didn't love me any more."

"But I did, Raissa, I loved you for *years*."

"Liar," she said affectionately. "It sort of bugged me. I'd gotten used to being adored by you."

"But you had a good life anyway. I can see that."

"It's had its moments."

"Did you have any children?"

"No, I hate kids. I must have told you that."

"Yes, I think you did. Come to think of it, I think you did."

The body never forgets, I suppose, and in leaning forward to talk to her I still felt, as I had at the end of things thirty years ago, that it was I who sought and she who gently rebuffed. I was in the presence of a woman who had left me, for whom I had stronger feelings still than she had for me. But I didn't care. She could leave the table, she could think what she wanted. *Poor Darius, still mad for me after all these years.* And I *had been.* Oh, that year in France, those midnight walks through that nasty brick city, the wind howling, the fine snow rising up from the pavement and swirling about like a ghost.

"Raissa, I was so lucky to meet you. Really, so lucky. It's like a dream to be able to say it to you."

"Yes?" she said cautiously, as if I might be making fun of her.

"No, no, I'm serious. I'm lucky to have had someone so beautiful to love when I was young. When I was so . . . *unappreciative.* Is that your husband?"

"Yes, I told you."

"Yes, so you did. He's very good-looking."

"Do you think so?"

"Yes."

"Slavic men age well. But you—you look just the same."

"Well, I'm used to it now, at any rate."

"I have a picture of you somewhere. I still have it."

"Oh God, don't show it to me. And how is your friend? I forget her name. Lydia?"

"God, you've got a good memory, Darius."

"For those days anyway. I couldn't tell you what happened last week if you put a gun to my head. Lydia *Zyrrba?*"

"Yes, I know who you mean."

"I always thought her name needed a couple of vowels."

"We don't see each other any more."

"I hope you didn't have a fight."

She shrugged. "Just one of those things."

"Raissa, can I ask you something?"

"Sure."

"That morning I saw you coming out of the apartment building—who was that guy? Did you end up with him?"

"For a while, yes. For six years actually."

"Good."

"Why good, Darius?"

"Just that that's a good long time to end up with anybody." I could see she was getting ready to leave. "Stay a second longer," I said.

"I'll see you again."

"Will you?"

"Yes. You know how it is: you don't see someone for a long time and then you run into them every day."

"Yes," I said, "that's true. That does happen sometimes." Involuntarily my eyes filled with tears.

"What, Darius? Don't be sad."

"I'm not sad. It's just that I haven't seen you in thirty years. I think if someone had said to me, it's going to be thirty years before you see her again, I think I'd have died or something."

"But you didn't, Darius, did you?"

I laughed and wiped my eyes. "No, apparently I didn't."

And then it *was* time for her to go. I stood up and put out my hand. She shook her head and, lightly brushing away my hand, kissed me on the cheek and held her lips to my face as if she were saying, I'm never going to see you again, Darius, and we both know it.

I didn't sit back down until she had disappeared from the doorway, this grey-haired woman who for a matter of months had lain in my bed and talked to me in the dark. We had known each other's bodies when they were young. How precious that was—for we held an image of each other which no one else in the world did, and when we died, that picture would exist no more.

The waiter rushed by with a bottle of wine for the next table.

Goodbye, Raissa, goodbye, my darling.

CHAPTER 11

When I was in graduate school, my roommate killed himself with a bullet through the temple. For reasons I've never entirely understood, his mother gave me the gun, with its almost full clip, at a reception after the funeral. I'm familiar with the saying, the arms maketh the man, but I was never tempted to use the gun, even in a rage, until one time in Chicago. It was a few years later and I was preparing for my orals, a crucial exam on the way to one's doctorate. I'd been up all night and had fallen asleep near dawn. In those days I was living in the university residence. Somewhere near seven in the morning I was awakened by a knocking on the door down the hall. Even though there was no response, it went on and on and on, until finally I got out of bed and looked out my door. Down the hall a long-haired young man, husky and dishevelled, was slumped backwards against the door, tapping backhand with his knuckles

whenever the spirit moved him. You could see from his physical posture that he'd decided to make a siege of it. He was going to bang on
the door until his friend, probably asleep or fornicating, answered,
no matter how long it took.

"Excuse me," I said, my voice roller-coastery with emotion,
"you just woke me up."

"Tough," he said, and just in case I had missed the point, he
swung himself around, this time leaning his face against the door
like a safecracker, and resumed his knocking.

Shaking with rage, I went back into my room and ripped open
my sock drawer and hauled out the nine-millimetre pistol. I lay it on
the night table and in so doing caught a glimpse of myself in the mirror. The colour had quite left my face. I ached to shoot him. To walk
briskly down the hall, to see his lazy, belligerent eyes come into
focus when he realized I had a gun at my side, to stop my trajectory
a few feet from him, to raise that same gun to eye level. What a
pleasure it would have been to see what Mr. Cool Balls would have
made of *that*. And if it didn't do the trick—if it, say, provoked some
unbecoming backtalk—then perhaps I could improvise a first-rate
pistol-whipping.

I didn't, of course. You can't pull a gun on someone unless
you're prepared to use it. And although I'm not a vulgar careerist,
even *I* knew that pistol-whipping a boy for waking you up in the
morning is a no-no when it comes to one's curriculum vitae.
"Excellent candidate except for episode with gun." Instead, I went
down the hall in the opposite direction to the bathroom and took a

hot, long shower, and when I emerged, my imagination still explod-
ing with violence, the guy was gone.

I confess the incident has stayed with me all these years and it
still bothers me. I wish I'd done something other than just *take it*,
that ponderous nonchalance. "Tough!" At least I wouldn't be still
thinking about it. I wonder, too, what ever happened to that boy. Did
he go through life knocking on doors until eventually someone *did*
give him a thrashing? Probably. That tends to be how things work
out. Pain, as they say, is life's only real instructor. But perhaps that's
just wishful thinking.

I mention this story for two reasons. First, to admit to a childish
tendency to hold on to ancient provocations, to roll them around in
my head for years sometimes, decades in this case, like a toxic marble.
Second, because, like Chekhov, I believe that you don't introduce a
gun into a narrative unless you plan to make use of it. Of that, more
later, I promise.

The truth is, even though I occasionally behave badly, I think
I'm a decent soul at heart, and so that business with Passion never sat
particularly well with me. I mean, good heavens, I took her to dinner, I invited her into my home—and she clipped me for everything
she could stuff into her bag. A shitty business indeed. But I didn't
retaliate. I couldn't, really. I had a hangover only a gun would cure.
(That word again.) One loud noise and I would have shattered,
hardly the sang-froid necessary to confront a pimp and his girlfriend. I also had the debilitating sensation that somehow I had had
it coming, that I had behaved like a sordid cretin and had got my

comeuppance. Mind you, that may have been a function of the hang-over. They're like that occasionally.

I wanted to let the whole thing go, I did, but I just couldn't. Sometimes, at odd moments in my day, I found myself thirsting for revenge, indulging in rather elaborately choreographed fantasies. Really, it was infuriating. I'd even offered to help with her customs agent's examination. Think of it—a customs agent! Passion going through your shaving kit, selecting who should and shouldn't be admitted into the country. What a perfect candidate.

Well, you see my point. It rankled me. But I've always tried to hold close to my bosom the adage that if you're going to do some-thing, wait until you're sober to do it. It doesn't matter what it is, a phone call to an old lover, settling an old score, whatever. The point is, I never thought of getting even with Passion until I'd had a martini or two; and then, in the warm light of my favourite restau-rant, near the end of the evening, I'd allow my imagination free play. But I never acted on it. I thought to myself, if you still feel like burn-ing down her house in the morning, *vas-y, fais-le*. But not tonight. Tonight, you should go home. And so I would. And invariably, I'd wake up in the morning and look back on the evening's final raging fifteen or twenty minutes and I'd feel a heavenly relief, as if I'd just stepped from the roadway seconds before an eighteen-wheeler roared by. Because in those twilight moments an act of violent retaliation made a kind of incontrovertible sense. It had its own compelling logic and, worse, an accompanying sensation that I was going to feel physically unwell *until* I took care of it.

I remember once, when I was a child, I was staying at a resort in South Carolina with my mother and older brother, now deceased. He was twelve and I was ten, and we'd had a spat on the beach, I can't remember what about, him teasing me about my big ears probably, but moments later my mother caught me slipping out of the kitchen with a steak knife. She stopped me, of course, I'm sure I knew someone would, but there was a moment when, knife in hand, I had tried to calm myself down but was unable to, feeling as if I would never again be able to breathe properly until I had committed this act. Until I'd terminated *with extreme prejudice* this lout who was too big to thrash by conventional means. It was as if a madman had taken temporary possession of my young body.

There were other episodes. I quit a summer job once because my boss criticized me at an end-of-day meeting in the office. Everyone was there. I can't remember what he said, but I remember hearing a faint snigger behind me. It left me with the sensation of having eaten poisoned food, a sensation I couldn't get rid of till I quit. Until I *acted* upon it. But I loved that job. I thrashed and tossed in my bed for nights afterwards. I was heartbroken. Finally I broke down and apologized. I got my job back. My God, the fuss! The point is, I knew *not to do it*, not to quit. I remember standing in front of the washroom mirror and saying, *Don't do this, don't do this*. But I couldn't stop myself. It was as if I were on a rail and once I started up, nothing, but nothing would stop me until I reached my destiny, no matter how ruinous. Which is a long-winded way of saying that I didn't think about Passion and her robbing me very often. But when I did, I did.

On the night in question I don't remember exactly when it started up, this psychotic choo-choo, but it must have been sometime after Raissa Shestatsky left the restaurant. I was too emotional to eat and kept stealing looks to see if the other diners might somehow have understood the magnitude of what had just happened. But the world went on as before. I wanted to batten things down a bit and ordered a vodka martini, which I drank greedily, then called for an encore. Before too long I had drifted into sleepy-eyed staring: the flickering blue light in a Moroccan restaurant, the blue-shirted employees in the Copy Shop across the street. Cars flowed by soundlessly on the other side of the window. At the conclusion of the second martini perspiration trickled under my arms and I had the curious conviction that it was snowing.

It wasn't. It was a balmy night and I dallied in front of the restaurant, unable to decide which way to go. I headed west, an unusual direction, pulled forward by the warm air and the blossoming vodka. It felt as if I were entering an almost holy state, the wind brushing my face and neck like a woman's fingers. I turned up a narrow lane. I didn't know where I was going, but I knew I was going *somewhere*. The noise from the main thoroughfare receded behind me, like someone shutting a car door from which music has been issuing. I was in Serrault's neighbourhood now, and it amused me to imagine for a second turning up at his door in this condition. He would certainly invite me in; he might well offer a coffee. But how fast a taxi would appear. What excruciating apologies one would owe after that. No, Serrault was a kindly man, but he was not the kind of man you dropped in on drunk.

It began to rain, a fine spray. I liked the sensation on my face. It was cooling, cleansing, as earlier that day something else had felt cleansing. What was it? Ah, yes, the notion of white tablecloths. Yes, there had been a purpose to that too—to get me out of the house, to get me to a certain restaurant at a certain time so that I might encounter Raissa. It had been a moment of clairvoyance. I had had them before, even as a child. That time my father broke his leg. The night a neighbour killed his wife. Or when my aunt Tullie called from California to surprise me on my ninth birthday, and I'd picked up the phone and said, "Aunt Tullie, where's my present?" By the end even my mother was a believer. She asked me once, "What's going to happen to me?"

"Nothing," I said. And I was right, you see. Nothing did.

When I had these moments, it wasn't at all like in the movies, where one appears to fall into a trance, sweat on the brow, murderous headaches, Vaseline on the lens, *ce genre de connerie*. Actually, it's quite a banal event; it's the *sensation* that's interesting. You see what's going to happen and it feels, in your body, as if you're *remembering* something. And not something very important either, more like where you left a book or an old telephone number.

It's also true that I never count the times I'm wrong. Those I write off as . . . Well, let me put it this way: you can't go looking for these things; they have to come in through the side door. When you go looking—when, as my gambling friends say, you chase the pooch—that's when you get things wrong. Wishful thinking has its own feel; you can mistake it for the real thing. No, it's got to just happen, which I know is uncharacteristic language for an academic, but there it is. Why, only the other day I'd had the impression of Emma's thoughts moving through my house like a group of frumpy women. It was as if they were on some sort of outing, a museum tour perhaps, these drab figures in shapeless coats going through my kitchen, picking up things, examining spice jars, commenting on cutlery, even on my French saucers (they were intrigued by them). They were *telling* me something, I knew that, but I couldn't decipher it. I tried too hard, I think, I was too obvious in my applications. Finally I knew that I had to glance away, just like that, I had to look away and concentrate on something else; and then, when I'd all but forgotten, when I had released my grip, I would suddenly understand, as if it had been whispered into my ear, what the grey women were saying.

Which brings me, involuntarily, back to that time when Emma moved out, the day of the clinking hangers. My goodness, not that again, I can hear you saying, and you're right. But bear with me. One final revelation. The truth is, I've never told anyone this, except Emma once, but by then her trajectory out of my life had acquired such momentum I'm not sure it even registered.

In those last two or three weeks she had arrived at some kind of resolution, that resolution being, forgive the jargon, that happiness is essentially one's *own* job, so to speak; and so the adolescent gloom which had hung over the house, rather like that of a teenager who has been denied permission for a weekend sleepover, lifted and there was again a freshness, a lightness to our life. And it was in the midst of this sunshine that she announced on that Sunday morning (why always on a Sunday?) that she was moving out. I always describe it as a shock, a surprise, which on a conscious level it was. But a few nights before—and a few nights before *that*—I had awoken at precisely four o'clock in the morning. Standing in front of the toilet, trying to pee, I had experienced a kind of horror, a premonition that something terrible was going to happen. I recall staring into the mirror and wondering, what is it? *What is it?* I thought perhaps I was going to be fired from my job or perish in a car accident. It never crossed my mind, never, not once, that it was about Emma, that she was going to leave me. One spends one's life preparing for tragedies that never happen; the real shockers, I now understand, the real knifings, always come at close range.

But you see, I knew something, as I did with the grey ladies in my kitchen, because when she finally made the quivering announcement that Sunday morning, *I can't live here any more*, I had a feeling, not of shock or surprise, but rather as if I were again remembering something. Suddenly I saw precisely what they had been pointing to, those night shivers at four in the morning. The roads were clear, so to speak, and the caravan got through.

Soon enough I was standing opposite the Village Health Spa. It glowed among the freshly budding trees like a sunken ship, its cabin still alight.

"Ah yes," I said in tones of bemused statesmanship, for I was again addressing the same audience that a drunk sometimes imagines is tailing him about town (how odd they have so little else to do). I stepped lightly off the sidewalk and crossed over to the other side of the street. (This provoked a small gasp of disapproval from the gallery. I could hear them stirring in their seats.)

Now look here, I protested, not a trace of a stagger, *pas même un soupçon*. I thrust my hands into my pockets. Trust me, my posture said, just a bit of fun and I'm off.

I mounted the curb and paused for a second, amused, open-minded, even a bit mischievous, as if I had just stumbled upon a student prank. A good sport. I had the sensation of pouting my lips as a Frenchman might seconds before he disagrees, or as you might prepare to kiss a dog. Rocking ever so slightly on the balls of my feet, I again heard the warning rumble of the cheap theatrical, Julius Caesar waving away the too insistent petitioner, but they were one and the same now, the stuffy spectators, the grumbling aluminum siding; they were emissaries from a more tentative world.

Playfully now (how sober I felt, how *lucid*), I peeked in the front window. A man in an appalling shirt sat behind the reception desk. With his salt-and-pepper hair he could have been a lawyer, but there was something of the gutter to him, something that implied a capacity for quick violence. And that shirt, green with red melons on it, the kind of thing a pimp might wear. I tapped at the window. He turned and, squinting in my direction, rose athletically and disappeared from view. A few seconds later I heard the front door open.

"Can I help you?" he asked.

"I wanted to see if you're open."

"Yeah, well, that's what the front door is for."

He went back inside and I followed him.

"I'm looking for someone," I said.

He nodded. Not an especially friendly nod. He appeared to be feeling along the inside of his teeth for a gap in which to rest the tip of his tongue.

"Does Passion still work here?"

He nodded. "She's busy."

"Busy for the night or busy for now?"

"Don't know."

"Should I wait?"

"That's up to you, sir."

*Sir.* There was something especially uninviting about the way he said it, as if an attack dog had been force-fed a few tricks of civilization, a ritual he was compelled to go through before being permitted his natural savagery. It struck me he'd learned it from the police, that tone of theirs when, looking about the inside of your car with a flashlight, they suddenly request you to step out. "Would you mind stepping out of the car, sir?" I wondered if he'd been in prison and looked down at his forearms for tattoos. But they were concealed by the sleeves of his dreadful shirt.

"Waiting will be fine," I said.

"That'll be thirty-five dollars then."

"For how long?"

"Half-hour."

"Do you want it now?"

"Yep."

"Not after?"

"House rules. Customers pay up front."

"I wonder why that is."

No response. Then, "So, what do you want to do here?" he asked.

I reached for my wallet. "Would cash be all right?"

"No, I want it in fucking *cherries*," he said.

I was taken aback by the sheer venom in his voice. But I was also just drunk enough to presume a certain customer impunity and said with some dignity, "One forgets sometimes that there are those people in the world who mistake politeness for weakness."

He hadn't the foggiest notion what I was talking about and it occurred to me that maybe he could smell the alcohol on me. In which case I could see very swiftly the portrait forming in his head, that of a rather sad-sack middle-aged man who, after a few bottles of wine, has screwed up the courage to buy what he could never have otherwise. Foolish as it sounds, it pricked my vanity that he might think that of me. Why would I care? I don't know. Only the other day I found myself bragging to an undergraduate about a book I'd published in my early twenties, the aftermath of which left me scratching my head with consternation. A certain hot shame dogged my footsteps for the next few hours. Why had I bothered? Surely by this point in my life I should have, I don't know, *outgrown* all that. Or at least the need for it. What was worse was that midway through my transparent crowing I had sensed that the undergraduate knew exactly what I was doing and his co-operative nods and little gasps of pretend surprise were entirely for my benefit, as if somehow he were looking after me.

Still, it annoyed me. I placed forty dollars on the counter. He put the bills thoughtfully in his shirt pocket.

"Casual accounting system you have here," I said. "Tell me, what percentage do the girls get?"

He gave his head a small shake, as if he were clearing it, which gave me to understand that it wasn't the question that confused him but rather the notion that it might be any of my business.

"Uh?" he said, widening his eyes, as if he had perhaps misheard me and was giving me the benefit of the doubt.

I repeated the question, my tone implying, I know you're a moron, so I'll go slowly. "How much do the girls get to keep of this?"

"All of it," he said.

"Oh," I said quite cheerfully, "that's nice. Can I have my change, please?"

"Sorry?"

"Five dollars. You owe me five dollars."

"Don't have it right now. You'll have to wait."

"What for?"

"I'll get it from another customer."

I looked around the deserted room. "No, I think I'd like my change now, please."

"I can't give it to you."

"Then I'll have to cancel the transaction."

He made no attempt to return the money, and in the tense silence I could see he was used to moments like this. And the thought crossed my mind, a man like this has punched people in the face before. And been punched. It's no big deal. I could feel my heart starting to pound. He went into the back and returned a few moments later with a five-dollar bill.

"That's very kind of you," I said with the fake friendliness one feels toward someone who has unnerved you. "Didn't mean to put you out."

"No problem," he said. It sounded as if he were warming up. Perhaps I'd misjudged him. Long hours, difficult clientele. Yes, I could see now how one might become a trifle brusque.

"And what's *your* name?" I said.

He paused for a second and you could see him pick it out of the air. "Donny," he said.

"A bit slow this time of year, isn't it . . . Donny?" I remarked. "It must be the rain. Canadians don't mind being cold, but they hate getting wet."

I repeated this little morsel of drivel as if I were saying it for the first time. It was in fact the hundredth time I'd remounted it, this rain-or-shine device to thaw unpleasant taxi drivers. But it failed to charm tonight. Donny was one of those creatures who feel no compulsion to smile at the jokes of others, a quality of coldness that chills me to this day.

"That a fact?"

"That is indeed a fact."

"So you want to go back or wait up here?" he asked, his interest in me at an end.

I thought for a second while his tongue again sought its niche.

"I'll wait in the back, Donny."

He led me down the hall, past a closed grey door where I heard muffled voices, a woman's laugh. It was Passion. He stopped in front of the second room.

"Knock yourself out," he said.

I wondered if I was supposed to tip him.

# 12

I closed the door behind me and sat down on the massage table. You could touch the wall on either side. Not enough room to swing a cat, but then again, why would one? The walls were a rich olive colour, surprisingly tasteful. A pair of pale cloth slippers peeked from beneath the table. The usual small nightstand in the corner, with its usual accoutrements, a box of Kleenex, baby oil, a candle, a clock radio, a box of surgical gloves for those clients in need of proctology. I peered into the wastepaper basket. It was filled nearly to the brim with squashed-up balls of tissue and from it, wafting upwards, came that slightly salty whiff one gets sometimes from certain trees in early spring, the smell of semen. How disgusting, I thought, how truly repellent in their *details* are the sexual habits of others.

I heard a door close. A man's chesty, self-assured laugh; the contentment of the freshly ejaculated. Cigar smoke, the voice retreating down the hall, then halting. Donny telling Passion she had a customer. The man's voice started back in, the tone different now, a winding-it-up voice. Donny must have given him "the look," let him know his time was up. *Sir.*

I was also aware that I had now come too far to turn back. There was no way out of the building except through the front foyer. No rear exit. A lapse in fire regulations perhaps; Donny would be on it first light for sure. I stood up quickly and faced the wall, my back to the door, pretending to examine a calendar for German chocolates. I stayed like that for I don't know how long, a minute maybe. She must have been washing her hands. Then very faintly there came a tapping of small knuckles on the door, and it opened.

"Good evening," Passion said brightly.

I turned around. The smile fell from her face.

"Hello, Passion."

"Oh, it's you," she said. Only a quick downward glance revealed the slightest uneasiness. In an instant she returned her eyes to mine like matching gun barrels. "I haven't seen you for a while."

"That's right," I said with pleasant surprise, as if I'd just noticed. I wasn't entirely sure how long to let these theatrics go on, but I was curiously aware that it required a certain effort on my part to remember that it was not *I* who had been in the wrong. It is a great skill of the psychopathic, I reflected, to make the offended party feel culpable.

"It *has* been a while," I said. Here I frowned and looked off toward the top corner of the room, calculating, it seemed, the months since our last encounter. I sat back down on the table. "How's school? You were studying to be a customs agent, as I recall."

"Oh that," she said. "I don't do that any more. Couldn't find the time."

"You're pretty busy now, are you?"

"Busy enough. And you? You still teaching?"

"Yes. Still teaching. Not much new to report there, I'm afraid."

She changed gears. "Okay, I'll give you a couple of minutes to get ready and then I'll come back. You like the oil, right?" This in the tones of a busy travel agent.

"Come to think of it, I *do* have something to report, Passion."

She stopped in the doorway.

"But you probably already know what that is," I continued.

She said nothing.

"What it is I have to report," I prodded her gently.

"No. What would that be?"

"Why, that would be *you*, Passion."

Careful pause. Always a chance one misunderstood. "Come again," she said with a trace of amused confusion. Brow furrowed.

"I'm going to report *you*."

"I'm not following."

"I'm going to report you to the police."

Like a sign on a roadside inn, which, after years of hanging by a single rivet, has picked that very second to crash to the ground, her bemused disguise fell the rest of the way off.

"Fuck off."

"Okay. I'll do that," I said briskly. "So you just hang about here for, I don't know, ten or fifteen minutes, and watch what happens." I stood up.

"Just a minute. Just a minute," she said. She stood in the doorway with her hands up. "What do you want?"

"I want my things returned."

"I don't have them."

"Where are they?"

"At a friend's. I don't even know if he's still got them."

How banal. And how obvious. I felt a wash of shame roll over me. My vanity, my stupid, craven, naive vanity. Of course it wasn't the first time she'd been to a client's house. This was a well-lubricated scam.

"Well, you better get on the phone." She seemed not to hear me. I raised my voice. "I *said* you better get on the phone—"

She shushed me.

"Is that your boyfriend out there?" I asked, referring to the thug in the blazing shirt.

"Don't get him back here," she said in a tone that alerted me.

"Okay then, we'll leave *Donny* out of it. Let me put it this way: I want my things back by noon tomorrow or I'm calling the police and they'll come here and they'll haul you—and *Donny*—away. Do you understand?"

She didn't answer.

"Do you understand?"

"Keep your voice down, I'm warning you."

I had the sudden, alarming sensation that I was out of my depth.

"Do you have my address?" I said.

"I forget it."

I pulled a pen from my jacket pocket and scratched out my number on the Kleenex box.

"By noon, Passion," I said, somewhat less convincingly than before, and stepped around her.

Donny looked up at me as I passed through the foyer. "Good evening," I said. He was watching me very closely, nodding his head almost imperceptibly. As I stepped outside I could hear him start down the hall.

It was half past three in the morning when the doorbell rang. I had been dreaming about a castle in Scotland, which I'd visited on my twelfth birthday. I was looking down from the top of the battlements. A row of damp flags drooped behind me. It was late afternoon; the sun hid behind a fog; the wet brown terrain ran straight down to the ocean; from somewhere out on the grey water came the sound of oars. I was bored. Holidays were always so boring near the end; how one hungered to get back to school. I felt in my blazer pocket for a cigarette, yes, there it was, and carefully, for its paper was wet, I extracted it. I tapped my trouser pockets: good, I had matches. I was striking the tiny colourless head against the cover when I caught sight of a woman in a window across the courtyard. She passed very quickly, like that. But that part of the castle was supposed to be empty. She must be a ghost! I must tell my mother that I saw Emma Carpenter in the window of a *castle*!

And then I heard the doorbell ring again. I got up, wrapping a towel around my waist, and hurried to the door. Holding the towel with one hand and pulling in my stomach, I swung it open. For a second I drew a blank.

"Donny," I said. "You're early."

He uttered something, a few words only, in a rather soft and not unpleasant voice, and I thought to myself, Ah, this is going to work out. I also realized I was still drunk.

"I'm sorry, what was that?" I asked, and leaned forward. But at that very second he grabbed my head between both hands and brought his forehead smack against mine. Red light exploded and I dropped to the floor, the towel fluttering to the side. He looked down at me with absolute calm. He's done this before, I thought. After waiting what seemed like a determined amount of time, like a man counting to ten before allowing himself to say something, he reached over and, putting his fingers slowly into my hair, grasped a handful and yanked.

"Do you want some more?" he said.

My eyes watered.

"Have you got any money in the house?"

For a wild second I thought there had been a grotesque misunderstanding, that he had somehow, the way things happen in dreams, mistaken me for somebody else.

"What?"

He pulled harder. "Money, fuckweed." His grip relaxed.

"I'm a pro*fessor*," I protested, and in the tone of my voice, its cowardly pitch, a moment from my childhood flared up like a match head, when a boy named Steven Love had backed me against the brick wall of my school and I had heard myself say, in precisely the voice I now heard, "I'm not *a'scared* of you."

"No safe, nothing like that?" he said.

"No, of course not."

He grabbed up the towel and pushed my head away, releasing my hair. "Wipe yourself."

I clamped the towel to my head.

He stood observing me for a moment. "A bleeder, eh?" You could see him thinking, like a slow reader turning the page of a book, as he moved to the next thought. "Jewellery?"

I shook my head.

He looked around the room. "I'm confused," he said. "Rich guy like you, buys his pussy, pays in cash. You got to have some money around here."

I sat up, holding the towel to my head. "I got it out of the bank today. Check my wallet."

He looked at me uncertainly. "Bank cards?"

I didn't answer.

"That's some split you got in your melon," he said, and he reached over and took me by the hand and pulled me to my feet.

I stepped away from him.

"Don't be scared," he said. "I won't hurt you." He kicked me in the shins, a short, sharp kick. I think he was aiming for my kneecap. I hopped away from him, but I tripped over my own feet. There was something slightly effeminate about it, the way I fell backwards with my hands out behind me, like a fat woman protecting her rear end. He's going to beat me to death, I thought.

"You sure you don't have a safe in here?"

I lay on the floor, my arm up. He leaned over. I could smell him. But he didn't strike another blow. He simply waited with this eerie patience.

Then, "You in there?" he asked. He smelt of cigarette smoke. "You listening?" He gave my ear a pull and smacked the top of my head. "You *listening?*"

"Yes," I said. "Yes, I'm listening."

"I'll be back tomorrow." He stood up. "Look at me," he said.

I was sure a kick was coming.

"Look at me," he repeated. He leaned over and yanked away my hand. It was shaking.

"Don't," I said. "Please don't."

"Get yourself to the doctor, I don't care, but I want to find something worthwhile here tomorrow when I come back." He toed me with his shoe. "You hear me?"

"Yes."

"What did I say?"

"You said you'll be back tomorrow."

"And what else did I say?"

"You want something worthwhile."

"Okay. Good. And Passion doesn't want to see you again. That relationship is *over*." He toed me again. "You got me?"

"Yes, yes, I got you."

"That all right with you? Answer me."

"Yes, fine, okay, I won't go back there."

He stood up straight, bending a little backwards as if he had a backache. "Well, I guess I'm finished here. What do *you* think? Am I finished here?" He took a deep breath and looked around. "Okay, we'll see you tomorrow, Professor. Noon sound good? Answer me. Noon's good?"

"All right," I said.

I went to the emergency room at Women's College Hospital, where an Asian intern put six stitches in my forehead. I told him I'd slipped on the bathroom floor, but he wouldn't have any of it. Automatically, as if it were printed on a slip that a machine had dispensed, he said, "You are too old to be fighting."

"I need some painkillers," I said. "My head is positively roaring."

He looked at me with appraising neutrality. "Have you been drinking recently?"

"How recently?"

"Were you drinking last night?"

"I had a glass of wine with dinner."

Instead of guffawing, he merely regarded me with a breathtaking lack of self-consciousness. "I can't prescribe painkillers if you've been drinking."

"My head is throbbing."

"I'm sorry."

"For heaven's sake."

He shrugged. "The problem with mixing alcohol and pain—"

"Jesus God, I don't need a lesson in pharmacology. I've just been whacked on the head."

"I thought you said you slipped."

"The floor. The floor whacked me on the head. It came up like this and it banged my head." I gave myself a glancing blow off the top of my head and, in doing so, cooked my own goose.

"I'm sorry," he said. "In the interests of your welfare I recommend you stay here for an hour or two. Until things settle down."

"Until what things settle down?"

"You could wait in the foyer. There's reading material. Perhaps even yesterday's newspaper."

This, I supposed, was as close to a joke as he was going to get. Now it was my turn to look at him neutrally.

"Forget it."

"Professor Halloway . . ."

"If you think I'm going to sit in your bloody waiting room with my noggin on fire and read the newspaper, you are as overworked as the newspapers say you are. There. How drunk could I be if I can manage a sentence like that without a stumble or a slur?"

"If you are still in discomfort tomorrow, you may return here and I'll give you a prescription for something."

When I got home I found the front door swinging on its hinges, dirt from the front garden hurled over the floor, a vase shattered. Someone had defecated in the kitchen sink.

Good God, I thought, reeling backwards, the smell making me gag, how did I get *here?* It struck me—for I suddenly saw myself as a man in the far corner of a photograph, irrelevant but fixed as such forever—that I was experiencing some kind of psychotic episode. I may even have said it out loud, *You are experiencing a psychotic episode*, but my heart was beating so fast I knew that very soon it wasn't going to matter whether or not I understood what was happening to me.

"You've got to slow things down," I said aloud, and to my surprise the sound of my own voice was quite reassuring. Even a hint of English exasperation, affectionate but firm. When I stopped speaking I noticed that everything began slowly to speed up again. My thoughts leapt forward. Little grey hounds, they were, dashing after the rabbit. But what exactly was the rabbit? Lord, what didn't I think of next? What unimaginable clutter! Poetry, shards of poetry, Corbière, Musset, Hugo, nothing good, nothing great, just the trash of too much reading, too much teaching, too much listening to the sound of one's own voice. And other things crowding around, standing too close, shouting "me too, me too, me too." That stupid quitting of my summer job. But why remember it now? It was more than thirty years ago! (This between the kitchen and the foyer.) I swore to myself even back then, I solemnly declared a hundred times after that episode, that the next time I arrived *here*, got caught on board a train that shrieks down the tracks, I'd remember not to *do* anything about it. Feel what you like, dream what you like, scheme what you like, but don't act on any of it. Leave it alone. Eventually it will just *go*, like dirty water running out of the bathtub.

And to be fair (here a wave of cheerfulness), for the most part it's worked. *La plupart du temps.* All those tranquil years in between. What tranquil years? What fucking tranquil years? What are you talking about? When were you tranquil? Was it not like having a beast in the basement catching its breath?

But no (despair ran over me again), it hasn't worked at all. I simply haven't felt like this since . . . since when? Since last time. Since the dogs. Those poor sad dead dogs. She must have thought they were sleeping. Yes, all right now, don't break my bloody arm, there were other incidents, if that's what you want to call them. That business with the steak knife and my brother. But be honest, who hasn't wanted to carve up his brother? What self-respecting younger brother hasn't tried, at least once? And so half-heartedly too. My goodness. And Raissa, of course, yes, that was a slightly, how shall we say, *energized* period, stalking about the city, weeping over *Madame Bovary* in a public park. Oh, and the tall Jewish girl, goodness, she threw me for a loop, Lord, yes, that was madness too. I didn't even *want* her.

Ah yes, I know what you're thinking, the addictive power of being loved, the third factor no one considers, you and me and it, just the three of us in such a small boat. But she left, you see, and, well, quite simply, I seem to be a chap who loves women who leave. *Quod est demonstratum.* It is their absolute, unmitigated, schizophrenic unavailability that makes them so precious. Indeed, who could be more desirable than an ex-lover crossing the street with a new man? Her coat swinging open, just a glimpse of all those treasures no longer within reach. Someone else's now. Yes, indeed, someone else's now.

And on it went, other episodes. How remarkable to have lasted so long, to have put up such a magnificent defence. A regular Maginot line. But why could I never—once the fit was upon me—see down the road to the point where none of this mattered, was the stuff of a port-and-cigars anecdote? *A bad patch, old chap, but I got through it,* and so on. Why the suc*cum*bing? It was as if my brain had turned against me, as if it had decided on its own to drive me mad. What does he need? Sleep? Then sleep shall be banished. Take it away. (A trifle grand, that, "to drive one mad." A bit kingly. Something perhaps less chest-thumping. To undo one. Yes, better.)

So there, now we understand one another. You haven't *gone* mad, you've always *been* mad. Small consolation, that. Hardly the prize at the end of the game show. Not exactly a new Chevrolet or a trip to Hawaii, this final persuasive knowledge that one has always been cracked, as they say in *Mad* magazine. Cracked. Hmm. Not exactly *le mot juste*. *Unhinged* seems closer to the point. Like a horse that won't stop running. No, *unhinged* isn't right either. What, precisely, is the word for a horse that won't stop running?

But stop it now. You are having a psychotic episode. But even as I said the words *psychotic episode* I knew it was a useless strategy. A furnace had suddenly clicked on in my brain and I didn't know how to turn it off. It would burn and burn and burn, it would agitate me for the rest of my life with its heat and speed and, worst of all, its *insistence*. Until it ran its course. Until I did something. Until I acted.

"Don't do this," I said out loud. "Don't do this." But it was such a weak voice, a tiny, ineffectual aunt whispering in the corner, "Wear your galoshes, dear. You'll catch your death of . . ."

Feel what you like, dream what you like, scheme what you like. But for heaven's sake, don't act on it.

I went down into the basement and shuffled through a box containing the early drafts of my master's thesis (*The Theme of Descent in Nineteenth-century Symbolists*) until I came across the clip from my former roommate's gun. I squeezed a bullet into my palm. It was half the length of my baby finger, with a brass casing. I ran back up the stairs, taking them two at a time, but a wave of dizziness caught me at the top and I almost blacked out. I steadied myself in the doorway for a matter of moments. Good God, I groaned, how did I get *here*? Why, only a week ago I was happy; I got up in the morning, I read the paper, I patted the cat, I went to work. And now look. Look!

I clicked the clip into the heel of the gun and cocked it once to put a shell in the throat. I looked up the barrel to make sure the bullet was in place. I couldn't see anything, but for a second there it looked like

I was going to commit suicide. *Committing* suicide. Yes, it certainly was a commitment.

I pulled a bottle of Javex from the kitchen cupboard and poured it over the feces in the sink. I had to look away and plug my nose. I turned the taps on full steam, I swished the nozzle back and forth, and soon it was all gone. I poured in more Javex and ran the hot water until the kitchen window steamed over, my brain still shouting poetry, *où le sceau de Dieu blêmit les fenêtres. Le sang et le lait coulèrent . . .*

Finally it was done. It was my sink again. Restored. One obstacle had been cleared. There was, it seemed, a checklist in my head and I didn't dare think farther down than the line at which I found myself at present. Out of the corner of my eye I could see it stretching onto a second page.

I pushed an easy chair in front of the main door, went back into the kitchen, and locked and double-checked the back door. Locked the door to the cellar. Fished through the kitchen drawers for a paring knife. Settled back on the chesterfield but only after checking the street again, north and south. Saw the red-haired woman whose dogs I'd poisoned. She came out of her house and got into her car. I wondered if she still thought about them, if she still missed them. Probably not. Probably fussing about something else by now. It would pass. Like the shit in the sink, it would be gone without a trace. A little, private episode. Really, how much of one's life is made up of these private incidents; how submerged one is. You know, for example, that you will recover from a broken heart, but somehow that piece of information, that *factoid*, never arrives at the soul or the brain or the nervous system, yes, the nervous system, where it might do some good. But if you know you're going to be all right, why then do you suffer so? *To get there.* To get where you know you are going to get to anyway. How pathetic, then, to feel good about having arrived. I survived, you say. Yes, but what else would you do? No one dies from love. Come, come.

I felt a curious urge—and with it a sense of impunity—to go into the street and tap on the red-haired woman's car window and say, It was me, I killed your dogs. My life back then seemed so . . . peaceful. What leisurely problems I'd had. A bark here, a bark there. Really, such a fuss *pour un rien.* Confessing, therefore, seemed rather an easy thing. It had been, on the face of things, rather a small crime when one came right down to it. The barking, not the killing.

But I didn't go into the street. I was far too busy. And besides, once one starts confessing, where exactly does one stop?

I took a deep breath. My, I was tired. Indeed, very tired. But I had work to do. I sat on the chesterfield and put on my reading glasses and took the paring knife and cut a deep "X" in the soft lead at the tip of the bullet.

"There, *Donny*," I said.

I went into the living room and knelt on the couch (where Emma had read *Anna Karenina*) and looked out the window like a child waiting for the rain to stop. By nightfall he still hadn't come. I went upstairs, the gun in my dressing-gown belt; stopped at the head of the stairs and looked back down the stairwell. I could feel a breeze blowing in through the crack in the broken door. I hurried back down to the basement, pulled out an old green banker's lamp, brought it upstairs, hooked it above the front door and plugged it into the foyer wall socket. Raced back up the stairs. Flicked on the hall light. Perfect, the lamp went on. Flick on, flick off. Perfect. Perfect. I could hear, clear as if an orchestra was playing on the front lawn, the opening, almost inquisitive notes of the *Concierto de Aranjuez*.

Darkness fell; the street lights had come on and I hadn't noticed; the sky kept its blue from the day, almost an aquatic blue, even though blackness lay over the streets and houses and lawns below. A full moon that looked as if it had been dispensed from a child's bed-time book hung in the sky. The red-haired woman came home. She walked up her front stairs, looking to the right and left, and there was something touching about her, these bird-like looks to each side, a fragility, a loneliness, as if she hoped at the last second to catch sight of someone on the street, a friend, even a neighbour, someone to chat to for a second before the house swallowed her up for another interminable, unfillable night. I wondered if she might be lonely without her dogs, and I felt a stab of regret. Such an odd, strange, sad, violent thing to have done, dead doggies on the grass, sleepy doggies . . .

Around two o'clock in the morning I heard a car door slam shut and I knew it was time. I hurried to the top of the stairs and lay on the floor. I listened. The car pulled away. Footsteps coming up the walk. The door creaked open.

"Professor?"

I turned on the banker's lamp. In the green light I could see him, silhouetted in the doorway.

"Go away," I said.

He shaded his eyes and looked up at me. "That you up there, Professor?"

I rested the butt of the gun on the floor and aimed it at his chest. Then he started up the stairs.

"I have a gun," I said.

"So do I, Professor . . ."

He turned his back to me; his shoulders went up as if he were reaching into the top of his pants. My behind contracted violently and I pulled the trigger. It was the loudest bang I've ever heard, like the end of the world, a flame shooting from the barrel. The impact spun him around. Catching the railing in his hand, he stepped down a few stairs, careful with his footing (so sad, that care), his knees buckled, he issued a loud groan and tumbled backwards, not flipping over but sort of sliding down the stairs headfirst, bang, bang, banging the back of his head until just his boots rested on the last stair and his heart, I guess it was his heart, sat on his chest. Right there, on his shirt, blown clean out of him.

CHAPTER 13

Don't worry, I'll get back to it. But indulge me for a second. Let me jump ahead, maybe a year, to an evening class where my future wife, who was taking a course in modern French poetry, introduced me to a longish short story. Now Chekhov, as I've learned, is an acquired taste; almost no one gets him the first time through, and for all their fussing I'm not sure the Russians ever have. *En tout cas.* She gave me this story, I now realize, because she was flirting with me. She had a crush on me not because I was handsome or brilliant, I was neither, but rather because I was her professor. Some people are just like that. Thank God. I was flattered. I tried to read the story, but it was flat and rather depressing, and I was just about to put it away when I came across the words "sparrow nights," a Russian expression, apparently, that describes a night of dementia and torment. When I came across those words, I didn't like it. Don't misunderstand me, I didn't feel compelled to kill her too, but it made me jump. For a few seconds I wondered if she was playing a kind of game with me, if maybe she knew what had gone on in my house that summer night and was giving me a bit of a wink. My Lord. A night of the sparrows indeed. Green smoke drifting through the air, cicadas chirping in the backyard. There was blood everywhere. Everywhere. I started to clean it up, but it was between the floorboards, between the kitchen tiles.

By morning I even thought of killing myself. I cocked the gun; the spent shell casing flew out and rattled onto the floor. I wrapped my lips around the barrel, but the taste of the metal and the cobwebs made one hesitate. Let us remember the *commitment* part of suicide. No getting up and walking away after that one. And then an extraordinary thing happened: I saw Emma Carpenter walking down the centre of the street. This was no hallucination. She was walking very casually, sipping a can of pop through a straw. I stood still as a snake. She didn't look over, but when she got abreast of my house, she dropped the pop can with a clank and threw out her arms. She stretched out those thin arms like Jesus Christ on the Cross and she drifted down the street.

I fell asleep. Mind you, I only slept for an hour, maybe a bit more, and when I woke up I was feeling a tad anxious. But it took a few seconds to remember why. Like a house of bricks collapsing on one, that was the sensation. It was, you see, exactly as I'd always dreamt it would be. I sat bolt upright. I jumped out of bed, I ran into the living room and there it was, indeed, a dead man on the carpet. Just like the nightmare. The thing I'd worried about happening had actually happened. And no gun either; he'd been bluffing. I, on the other hand, looked, well, rather bad, to say the least. The banker's light over the door, the dumdum shells. The bullet in the back—they would gas me for that one alone. Just remember, I told myself, you can always kill yourself later.

I dragged the body into the kitchen. I dragged it back into the hall. I did everything but put a lampshade on its head and ask it to dance. I dragged the poor bugger down the stairs, *bang*, *bang*, *bang*, went his head. I tried to stuff him in the furnace, but his shoulders were too wide.

I showered and I remember snapping open the shower curtain a half-dozen times, expecting to see a blood-spattered Donny in the bathroom doorway. Finally I left the curtain open altogether. But the body. I had to do something about the body.

I had an old-fashioned furnace, an oil burner, with a big door; you could open it and see the flames inside. But it was too narrow by six inches. So I did what you would do. I didn't call the police, I didn't put a gun in my mouth. I dried my hair under the hair dryer, things moving rather rapidly, shaved, brushed my teeth and took the street-car—for some reason the streetcar seemed less suspicious, less the act of a guilty man—out to the identical hardware store where I had bought the rat poison. I bought an axe and a tarpaulin and putting them in a taxi—one doesn't carry an axe on the streetcar—I returned home. When I lifted Donny onto the tarp, I noticed a wallet in his back pocket, attached to his belt by one of those silver chains. I pulled it out and opened it. Donny Most, that was his name. What a strange name. I stuffed it back under the body and then stood up and took a deep, deep breath. This part is not very pleasant, so skip ahead if you want, but it had to be done. I chopped his arms off at the shoulder. And then he fit. I stuffed him headfirst into the furnace, clothes, boots and all, and tossed his arms in after. Then I shut the door, went upstairs, turned up the thermostat to ninety and opened all the windows on the ground floor. I heard the furnace go on below. Then I went out and sat in the park. It was a lovely spring day, but there was something wrong with the colour of things, as if my attention was so electrically focused on the body in my furnace that it quite drained the colour from the world around me. It reminded me of Emma, actually, of those days when I wandered around in the spring sunshine waiting and waiting and waiting for the phone to ring. The world had looked like that then too.

So I sat in the park on a bench. It was the same bench I had kissed Emma Carpenter on, that summer night a hundred years ago. An old woman sat beside me. For a second I thought of striking up a conversation with her, but I was afraid I smelt of alcohol and I didn't want her to remember me for any reason at all. So I sat silently, watching a cat batting a flower with its paw. A gentle wind blew across the park; it was coming from my house and I thought for a second I could smell human flesh burning. It struck me like a blow in the chest. I looked over at the woman. Could she smell it too, Donny burning up in my furnace? People say that human flesh smells like chicken when it's burning and that's precisely how it smelt. It made me very uncomfortable until it occurred to me that it *was* chicken, that somebody was having a barbecue in a backyard. I could feel things starting to speed up again, and by now the world around me had turned almost black and white, the colour sucked from the grass and the budding trees, everything the colour of dirty swallows. I thought about going to the liquor store for a bottle of bourbon, but—and I know how this sounds—I was afraid of getting drunk and doing something foolish. But that smell, that burning chicken.

Finally I couldn't stand it any more. I went for a walk. I walked all the way down to the lakeshore. I ran into Serrault in Kensington Market. I nodded rather formally. It was uncharacteristic of me; I tend to lean toward the excessive when greeting people, if only to show I'm not frightened of them, but Serrault noted I was out of form and, with a private smile (such good manners), steered his boyfriend into a cheese shop. I took the back streets after that, but it didn't help. It was one of those peculiar days when you run into everyone who ever made you uncomfortable but whose feelings you don't want to offend. So I just kept waving and smiling, never breaking my stride, the way I've heard movie stars do.

I got down to the CN Tower. I walked all the way across the parking lot and touched it with my fingers, like it was home base, the way you do when you're a kid, and then I went into a small bar a few hundred feet away that overlooked the train yard. It was a rickety little joint, only a half-dozen tables, and I sat by the window. I hadn't had a beer in fifteen years, but I did that day. And I liked it, big and frothy, and oddly comforting, just the bulk of it, and for about thirty seconds, partway through the second pint, I felt my shoulders come down and I yawned. I *yawned. Tu m'entends?* But it didn't last. I could feel my thoughts beginning to hurry on the way home. I resisted the temptation to run the last few blocks just to get it over with, a terrible, chest-constricting urgency compelling me forward. But when I cleared the top of my street, expecting to see police cruisers and yellow tape wrapping my house like a last-minute birthday gift, I saw nothing but a quiet street on a spring day. I started across the park I'd crossed that day Emma left me. I think I even stopped and stood on my tiptoes to see if there was anyone on my porch. No one. Not a soul. I walked by the house, stealing a look at the front door. You could hardly tell it was busted and for a second, a dream second, I hoped . . . well, you can imagine what I hoped. But then I saw a split in the wood near the doorknob and I knew the whole thing was true.

I didn't go in. I couldn't face, not for the moment anyway, the thing in the furnace. So I kept walking. I walked all the way up to Dupont and I went to the beer store. It was Saturday afternoon, the place full of men in baseball hats, their cars pulled up with girlfriends in the passenger seats; old men bought little six-packs and took them home to rooming houses. I ordered a dozen long-necked beers. Something about their shape relaxed me. I must have seen someone somewhere drinking one, down in Mexico, someone young and easy. I carried them down the street on my hip, like homework. My Australian neighbour was in his driveway, lying under his car, tinkering, but his radar was so sharp he detected me and scrambled out.

"Having *another* one of those days?" he asked, and I replied with a roaring laugh. Really, it sounded like a car backfiring. But I was loath to provoke trouble—some days one sees the world as a potential character witness—and I stopped for a few moments for a chat. But I could see I wasn't pulling it off. I was running on a kind of octane, which, because I'd been in my own company for so long, had begun to seem rather normal but when out in the world must have struck people as . . . somewhat off.

"I'm having a bout of insomnia," I said, hoping that might explain the rather driven look of my features. The skin on my face seemed a size or two too small for my skull, as if in washing it the night before, it had shrunk like a new cotton shirt. I made my excuses, laughed wildly at a parting remark of his, and hurried home, head down, praying not to encounter the woman with the red hair. Today would be the day, if such a day existed, that she would confront me with the killing of her dogs, and I was sure I'd shatter like a vase.

I closed the door behind me and went into the living room and sat on the couch and opened a bottle of beer, still cool from the chiller, and drank it rapidly. It was only a few seconds before I again had the impression of momentary calm, as if the situation was somehow deal-able-with. Knowing, as I did, that this was probably a trick, still I toyed with the idea of how I could prolong it—if only for a few weeks—until habit set in, until the thing in the furnace became merely *one* of the facts of my life. Albeit a king-sized one. A jumbo concern, so to speak. Until then what I needed to do was stop myself from acting, from responding to wave after wave of panic, the acting out of which would almost certainly ruin my life. Well, easily said indeed.

Still. Going to the police now was obviously out of the question. They would throw a butterfly net over me and I would remain under it for twenty-five years. But after my clumsy experience with my neighbour I knew I had to stay out of the public eye for some time. Until I stopped looking and behaving like an escaped animal.

Lord, it was hot. I realized after a few moments the furnace was on. I turned it down. I heard it click. The house fell silent. I phoned the French department and left a message on the answering service; a bout of strep throat, I said, be off a week, want to give you all plenty of notice. Pip, pip, consummate professional and all that. Then I got down to business. I washed the living-room floor; I washed the kitchen floor; I cleaned up the shattered vase. I was very thorough. But things were again going way too quickly, more avalanches of poetry and old songs from high school and shouts from boys I'd known in university. Lord, the sound of a boy's voice across a cricket pitch at sunset. How haunting. *Darius, come with us. We're going to the pub. Do come!* I checked my watch. It was after five. The sun over the yardarm. Safe to have a drink now. An honest day's work behind us. Oh yes, let's not flirt with trouble; perhaps, I reasoned, today is not the day to address whether I do or do not have a drinking problem. I went to the fridge and got a beer and put two in the freezer and then came back and put my feet up on my desk and stared out the window. It was a spring evening. I drank the beer, then one from the freezer. So cold, it was like putting out a fire. I held it to the side of my face. My God, I must have a fever.

I was drinking the third beer when my eyes fell on a photograph, a framed black-and-white picture my Spanish roommate had taken of me in France that year I lived in Toulouse. He had caught me sitting at the dining-room table, looking up a word in a dictionary of Old French, and I'd looked up at him and smiled, but you could see by the smile—or I could—that I was distracted. I had been reading *La Chanson de Roland* (in the original, I add snobbishly) at that very moment, but what I had really been doing was thinking about Raissa Shestatsky. Even though there was precious little to think about, at this time every evening in Toulouse a kind of anxiety about her had clutched my young chest, as if she might just be starting the evening, getting ready to go out and meet her boyfriend, everything moving toward that midnight point where they would go back to his apartment and make love, my lovely naked Raissa on her hands and knees . . . my sacred, lovely, inviolable Raissa. But looking at the photograph, I raced ahead months to the coffee we had when I got back, to the strange yawn that had interrupted the story she was telling, that had signalled my heart's end to her. Looking at my worried, anxious face in the photograph, I realized that if I could only stop from self-destructing over the next little while, if I could just keep a lid on this body in the furnace, I had a chance of returning to earth. I had survived Raissa; I could survive this.

To that end I rose quickly and went into the medicine cabinet, took my entire supply of sleeping pills and flushed them down the toilet, not without, at the last second, a moment's terrible doubt that almost threw me to my knees in an effort to suck the water from the toilet bowl. I may even have contemplated disassembling the water pipes in the basement and licking their insides. But the body was down there and I wasn't prepared to go down those stairs to find a bloody and intact Donny, somehow rescued from the oven, standing, his heart in his hand, in the dark, waiting for me. No.

Still, a murder is a murder is a murder. But (this on the third beer), when you come down to it, it *is* only a number. Another missing person. And not a very nice missing person at that. Would Passion come looking for him? Doubtful. Doubtful that she even knew he had come back a second or a third time. Would she call the police? Very, very unlikely. Not that, over the next three months, I might not wake up in the middle of the night, sweat-soaked and certain she would. Looking at the photograph of myself, I again felt a wave of reassuring exhaustion, so profound my head slumped forward and I dozed in my chair, my feet still on the desk. I roused myself, took a pee and collapsed on my bed, fully clothed.

I awoke to a foul smell. It was my own body. I was sweating like a madman. My shirt was wet. Even my pants around the rim of my waist. Mechanically, like a dream walker, I went to the top of the stairs. I fingered the bolt. No, I was not prepared for that yet.

I showered, again leaving the bathroom door open—the shower curtain as well. Moments later, imagining a flurry of furious knocking at my door, I stole from under the water, leaving large damp footsteps on the wooden floor. I peeked out the living-room window at an angle where I could see the front door. No one. The shower ran on, sounding again like the agitation of unhappy soccer fans.

"You need to eat," I said, my voice dry, as if I had not spoken for a long time. But when I found myself on the porch, I listened for a second and, catching the reassuring sounds of the furnace humming in the bowels of my house, I headed north, up my street but away from the restaurants. I climbed a steep flight of stairs through the back of Casa Loma and in the growing dark crossed over a long bridge. My God, what an evening, the sky turquoise, airplanes floating silently overhead like a string of fireflies, one after the other, floating over my head and the bridge and the park that spread out damp and dark below me. An evening to weep for.

A woman walking a dog passed me on the sidewalk. I wanted to say something to her, something to share this breathtaking evening, but I didn't. I suspected it would frighten her. The planes passed overhead and I thought, yes, that's it, I'll take a trip somewhere. I'll take a trip to a Caribbean island and when I come back . . . I stopped in my tracks. But what if, while I was away, someone were to come to my house? Were to see the broken door? They might think I was inside, ill or dead or murdered. Call the police. The police would look around. *Hello, what's this in the furnace?* No, I must get the door fixed first.

I walked slowly over the bridge, the air cooling my overheated body; cars rolling across the bridge, headlights on now, the hum of rubber on cement. All heading downtown. Dinners, dates, families . . . My goodness, how lonely a thing this—this *incident* has become. And this is the punishment, no doubt, the dreadful, incommunicable solitariness. A reason to turn oneself in, to extinguish this furnace in the brain. This drifting about the world like a ghost. And that image: a man wobbling on the stairs, as if he were on the verge of telling you something, as the sensation *I am dead* sinks in, like a straggling soldier returning to the fort. How sad, that momentary eagerness when, yes, he did look as if he'd remembered something, his brain mistaking the real message, hoping perhaps it was another. How sad to see a creature, even *that* creature, in such distress. But why did he say he had a gun? Would it have mattered? Wouldn't you have shot him anyway, coming up the stairs like that, a thrashing in the works for sure? Why, he might have shot you with your own pistol. No, you would have done it anyway; you couldn't have that crashing up the stairs and not fire. A child would have fired. There had been no doubt, not at the moment, not the second of the big squeeze. Still, if only he'd had a gun, how much better things would have gone. But he didn't. And there's an end to it. Perhaps I could have found one. Popped it into his hand. But which hand? No, no, no, no, no. It's always the extra lie that hangs you. The unnecessary elaboration. Sin boldly and be done with it. But this solitude, this unspeakable solitude and the notion of it spreading out over years, like an ever-widening ink stain, made me think for one second of hopping over the side of the bridge. But come now, you can kill yourself anytime, there's no rush on that one.

I turned. A man in a bowler hat was standing right behind me, waiting to pass on the sidewalk. I hadn't heard him come up.

"Good heavens!" I said. "You frightened me!"

He tipped his hat and stepped around me, a jaunty man in a long dark raincoat. I watched him get to the end of the bridge and disappear into the park.

I kept walking up Spadina, up and down a hill, past the Russian consulate and into Forest Hill Village. Oh yes, there it was, the kitchenware shop where I'd once bought an especially sharp carving knife. But the knife was gone now, Emma had taken it. Curious how materialistic she'd been on the way out the door. She'd taken the cutlery, half the coffee mugs, even the duvet we'd slept under that whole winter. Yes, she'd paid for it, but still, an odd thing to want in her new apartment, if she wanted a new start. Did she at least have it dry cleaned? The night she came to fetch her possessions (months after the end) I'd left the house, I remember. I didn't want to watch her get her things, her brother hovering protectively in the doorway as she went from room to room, opening drawers, looking under the bed, peering up into the cupboards. No, I certainly had no need to see that, the two of us chirping small talk, school, classes, eccentric mutual friends. What a horror that would have been. Worse than death. But no, one says that, worse than death, but in fact it wouldn't be worse than death. It would be quite a bit better than the thing with the singed cowboy boots in the furnace. Now that was a horror. Anyway, when I came back that evening, the night she finally took away the last of her things—She had taken her underwear the first day, had wanted to spare me the weepy humiliation of plunging through the laundry basket at three in the morning just to find a trace of her . . . and I would have too. A considerate young lady. Almost a year after she'd gone I woke up in the middle of the night, it was winter, cold and still, the window frosted along its base, and I suddenly remembered the existence of a small chest of drawers, useless really, that I had set behind a glass sliding door in the guest room. And in the second drawer from the bottom I knew, I absolutely *knew* there was a piece of her clothing that I had seen her put there three, four years earlier. How perverse a brain I have, how sick of it I am; how dangerous a thing it is to have waited for so long, to have lulled me into a sense of false security, only to wake me up at the hour when one is most alone and least protected from one's imagination, and to have sicced, like a dog, that foul image on me. I got up and went down the hall to the guest room and slid open the doors, *crash*, and yanked the blanket off the set of drawers and pulled open the second-from-last drawer, and there it was, the small white T-shirt with a hole under the arm. And that T-shirt seemed to contain the very spirit of her, her slimness, her dirty-mindedness, her infinite and forever gone desirability—so much so that I got dressed and took the T-shirt and went downstairs and out onto the still and snowy porch and lumbered across the street in my bedroom slippers into the park and dumped it in a garbage can and covered it with a newspaper. And the next day when I headed down to Bloor Street to do my shopping, I couldn't help myself, I cut through the park and peeked into the garbage can with the trepidation of one who expected to see a coiled cobra there. The T-shirt was gone . . .

But where was I? Oh yes, the night she took her things. I came back to my house after midnight and I saw in the light from the street the glint of her keys lying on the carpet just inside the door.

She'd locked up and taken them off her key chain and dropped them through the mail chute. Lying there on the carpet, they were indeed the last of Emma. Keys I will no longer need in this life. I picked them up off the carpet, I looked at them, I even smelt them. But they were dead. They carried nothing of her.

Anyway. Up in Forest Hill, the kitchenware store was still open and for a second I thought of going in and buying another paring knife. Perhaps not. Perhaps wandering the streets with a knife was not such a good idea after all. I moved on. I glanced inside a restaurant, but it was too empty, the waiters clustered in the corner, listless, too keen to pounce. Besides, waiters don't like single diners on a Saturday night. I could imagine the tall one in the pressed white shirt snapping open my table napkin with a chilly *politesse*, assuming, already, that my table would yield little of remunerative interest. Perhaps he saw me as a lonely widower who wanted to chat. How dull for him.

I went into a Japanese restaurant and sat at the bar between two couples, one my age, the other on a first date. I ordered a Kirin. It was lovely and went straight to my head, and then I ordered another and I could feel a sort of swagger coming on, as if my life and the events of the last twenty-four hours were assuming a mythological posture. As if I were a rare adventurer.

I left the restaurant and, moving east, drifted through the darkness and the opulent lawns and the grand mansions and the living rooms in which families hovered like expensive goldfish, all the while conducting a conversation between myself and an imaginary companion whose grinning admiration egged me on . . . Really, it was quite insane, and I rather had a sense of it being insane, stopping, as I did, to pee in a giant mulberry bush. But still it kept on in my head, this *histoire de moi*, until I reached Yonge Street and something changed. There, under the naked lights and the slightly worn-out feel of the neighbourhood, a place that had peaked twenty years earlier, I experienced a twinge of worry, a tugging at my sleeve, a sense that I was walking on a very narrow ledge on either side of which lay some very bad things. I sped up my pace. It was a mild night, the sidewalks teemed with people, but the notion of running into someone I knew filled me with the most awful dread (even though it had been my hope for company, for distraction, that had drawn me out of the shadows) and I turned up a dark street. Like a reptile slipping into its pond I felt a momentary relief, a coolness. But I couldn't slow things down. I cut across a dark park and as I neared a set of empty tennis courts I found myself, for the first time in many years, praying. I promised God that if he'd take away this sensation, this feeling of almost electrical urgency, I would . . . what? I cast about in my deepening inventory of suicidal vices—they *all* seemed suicidal at that moment—and grabbed the pot with the longest handle. I'd stop drinking. By the time I got to the end of the park I was almost running. By now I was talking to my mother, as the wounded and the dying do, I was begging for comfort, just this last once, this last time. Put your cool hand on my brow as you did when I was a little and had a fever and you came in the middle of the night and tucked me in. Sometimes she would take off all my blankets and then one by one waft them back over me; first the sheet, she'd lift it up again, and it would flutter down, so cool, so clean. How happy children can be in their beds.

CHAPTER **14**

My house was an inferno, but I didn't dare turn off the furnace. I saw my salvation, my escape, in every second it roared. I closed the heating vents in my bedroom, shut the door and opened all the windows in the house. Outside in the back garden, the way one always catches sight of the macabre at a time when one can least cope with it, I saw my neighbour's yellow cat with a mouse in its mouth; you could almost hear its tiny screams. Lord, what a world.

The bathroom was windowless. I ran a bath for myself, the steam rising from the water, tricklets of sweat running down my chest as if I were in a tropical country. I turned out the overhead light and lit a candle; the odour of black cherries filled the overripe air. I slipped into the water and rested my feet on each side of the faucet. I inhaled deeply. I observed with more than a passing sense of irony that I had finally turned my own home into hell. *Vous êtes enfin arrivé!* I watched my chest rise and fall in the water, my heart thundering. We have to find a way to slow things down. Everything is bearable but not at this speed. I looked at my watch. Ten-thirty at night. Give it till one o'clock. There's always last call. Have a quiet pint or two at a corner table. Attract no attention. Then, if the willies come in the night, there's beer in the fridge. We can ease this thing down, we *can*. I took a deep breath. What is this? A trace of fatigue, a trace of letting go? What happens if we do nothing? What happens if we just stay here in this—I looked about the room, the walls dripping with perspiration as if they themselves were sweating—*greenhouse* until sleep comes? Until sleep comes down like snow.

I yawned. Heavens. Banished sleep sneaking in the side door? Perhaps my body will simply give up on its own. Merely a question of waiting it out. A siege of one's own body, waiting for it, like that Scottish castle, to surrender, to run up a white flag, to say, He's serious this time, boys, we're not getting any more of anything. I got out of the tub, the squeak of my behind on the porcelain. Damp-footed through the house, opened the door and quickly slipped into my bedroom. Lit another candle. Listened to the night sounds. A boy bouncing a basketball in a side street . . .

At three o'clock I woke up with a start. I looked at my watch. I had been dreaming about reading again, that I should put my book down before I rolled over and crushed it; and now it turned out I had been sleeping all along. I had been *asleep*! I had been to that foreign country! I rolled over. My pillow was damp; my sheets were damp. No matter, no matter. All that could be fixed. There was a sort of sensual pleasure in it all, and I began to summon up images of

Emma. How safe an island that was now. How without pain the voyage was now. Emma in a movie theatre, her white hand under her skirt. Just a second, she whispers, staring straight ahead at the screen; even now she can't take her eyes away. I have a little present for you, she says. There. Do you like that? Is that what you wanted? Now sit still and watch the movie. Emma! Emma!

But wait. There was something wrong. It seemed to me that seconds before I woke up I had heard a click. Yes, definitely a click. But what was it? I lay still for a moment, staring at the ceiling. The furnace. The furnace had stopped. Someone had reached a hand onto the thermostat and turned it sharply to the left. I opened my bedroom door and looked out. The house was cool and in the moonlight I made my way through the hall and into the living room. In the light from the street I saw the thermostat glow dully. But I had forgotten my glasses. I reached out a hand and touched the dial. I turned it ever so slowly to the right. Turning, turning, turning, waiting for the sound of the furnace going on below. The dial reached its apex with a soft click. Nothing. The furnace had run out of oil. How in God's name was I going to fill it again? How could I have an oil truck come to my house in the last days of April without alerting the neighbours, without saying, in fact, I have a body in my furnace and he's *not quite done*! Parsimonious prick that I am, always doing things in half measures (except Donny, of course, no half measure there). Skimping on oil, filling half the tank, paying half my bills, doing half a novel, half a poem, everything in unmatching halves. Like a bloody prop room for a little theatre company, my life was. Mismatched everythings. I went back to bed.

When I woke up again it was grey daylight, and I hurried downstairs and looked out the front window. It was snowing. I went to the door. My eyes went involuntarily to the crack in the wood the same way that one watches *Romeo and Juliet* with the irrational hope, even though one has seen a hundred different productions, that this time out the Nurse's message will arrive on time.

This was no hallucination. It was indeed snowing. I could even smell it. An odd snowfall, too, tiny white balls, like spitballs, the kind kids blow through a straw, falling in a perpendicular line straight down to the earth. As if they were being poured from a huge basket. The snow gathered in the bows of the trees, on my front gate, on the lawn, and with it, it seemed as if God were handing me a break.

I called the oil company. In a voice tremulous with emotion—perhaps they thought I was horrified by the weather—I complained that I'd run out of oil, the house was freezing. I even invented a child, yes, I have a child here, shivering over his cornflakes. Fine then, excellent, send your best man. You would have thought I was ordering fresh troops to the front.

An hour later a fat, dirty oil truck stopped in front of my house amidst a scream of hydraulic brakes. I opened the door in my dressing gown and sent the driver around the side of the house. Soon one could smell the rich, comforting scent of fuel oil wafting up from the basement. I prepared my cheque book, wrote out the name of the company and waited patiently on the chesterfield. The doorbell rang and I went to answer it. While I was filling in the amount,

I heard the driver come into the front hall.

"Which door leads to the basement?" he asked.

A hand clutched at my heart. "May I ask why you're asking?"

"You may ask," he said, and truncated the sentence with the swiftness of chopping off an arm. A shot of electricity stiffened me. I opened my mouth and to my horror nothing came out. Tantamount to a confession. Christ, even the neighbours must have heard it, the sound of an axe severing the tendons in Donny's shoulder. The oilman smiled a wide, rural smile, and I realized he was making a joke, not a terribly funny joke but the sort of thing a fireman might find amusing, although I can't say why I thought of firemen specifically. He made a jumpy little motion with his hand as if he were brushing crumbs from an invisible table, a gesture that suggested we simply *must* excuse him, he was quite the "character."

"You were saying?"

"I got to light the pilot. When you run out of oil, the pilot light goes out."

"So you need to do what exactly?"

"Well, give me a match and I'll show you."

"Why don't you just tell me."

"It'll be easier if I show you."

"Look, I don't mean to be rude, but I don't want a stranger monkeying around in my house with a match and a full tank of oil. So tell me, what do you have to do?"

"There's a little gizmo on the side of the furnace—"

"On the *side*, you say?"

"You have to light it."

"From the *side?*"

"Yes."

I softened my tone. "Okay then. I hope you don't think I was being untoward."

"No problem. Lead the way."

Astonishing. A utility man without a chip on his shoulder. Remember to tip him. I led him through the kitchen, catching sight of a streak of dried blood six inches above the floorboard. How had I missed that? What else had I missed? I unbolted the door and heard him clump down the stairs behind me. I took him over to the furnace and stood in front of its door.

"Do you have a light down here?" he said.

"No, I'm sorry. I'm afraid it burned out."

"That's okay," he said cheerfully, almost gratefully, because it allowed him to pull a small flashlight from a shirt pocket. A thin beam bounced around the room, settling on the furnace door. "Hey, she's an old one."

I didn't budge. "Where did you say the pilot light was?"

He went to the side of the furnace and opened a small portlette. Holding the flashlight in his teeth, he lit a cigarette lighter and held it in the hollow. A small whine ensued, like a propane lighter that hasn't caught.

"That should do her."

I had turned my back to him and started up the stairs when I heard a dreadful sound, the squeal of the furnace door opening.

"What are you *doing?*" I cried. But it was too late. He was peering into the furnace.

"Just checking to see she took." He poked around with his penlight. "But what's this?"

I came up quietly behind him. "What is what?"

He stuck a gloved hand in the hole and withdrew a black object. I couldn't see what it was. A foot, a hand, a shrunken skull. He held it under the light.

"It looks like *a* axe head."

He'd done this twice already, dropped the consonant before a vowel, and I wondered if he did it on purpose, if it was part of being "a character."

He turned the object over in his hand. "It is. It's *a* axe head." He showed it to me.

"Do you do that on purpose?" I asked, referring to his grammar. But he appeared not to be listening.

"Now how in the hell did that get in there?"

"It's *a* old furnace," I said.

A small smile betrayed him. "You thought I was jerking you around, eh?"

"Never. Never."

I followed him back up the stairs and into the front foyer. He looked at the door. Went over and fingered it.

"Had a break-in?"

"Yep."

"Cops come?"

"You bet."

"Say, where's your son? I heard you had a child here."

"He's doing his homework."

"On a Sunday?"

"He's a good boy."

"I never did my homework till Sunday night. That is, if I did it at all."

By now I was, I confess, eyeing the brass candle holder on the foyer table.

"There's more to life than just homework," he informed me, and I nodded with slow appreciation.

"Indeed," I replied. I opened the door. "Hang on," I said and, against my better judgment, hurried back into the kitchen and took a ten-dollar bill from the coffee mug on the fridge. I handed it to him, turning my wrist slightly as if it were a secret hand-off.

"Oops, can't tell my boss about that," he said.

"Don't worry." I looked at his vest. "*Lainie.*"

He looked up at the sky. "Snow's stopped." He stood in the doorway, looking upwards, giving it—or something—deep reflection. "Just goes to show you," he added, and then started down the walk.

Remembering "The Cask of Amontillado," I resisted the temptation to ask him what exactly I was being shown. Then with a solemn nod from the cab, Lainie withdrew from the neighbourhood.

CHAPTER 15

During my undergraduate year in Toulouse, I was frequently broke, and that Christmas a distant aunt sent me a money order in lieu of a present. But she sent it to the wrong city, to the Crédit lyonnais in Marseilles, which was some three hundred and fifty miles away. News of the mix-up got to me on a Thursday afternoon, a four-day holiday beginning the following afternoon at two sharp. My irritation, not to mention my self-pity, kept me tossing in my bed until sometime after midnight, when I leapt up in a shaking rage and decided to hitchhike to Marseilles. It was an extraordinary night: the small towns, the smell of the ocean, the bleak stretches of highway at four in the morning. But such an adventure, such a quickening of my spirit. I had a job to do, a place to be, and a deadline. A real one, this time.

I was young, I had a friendly face and I made it to the bank by ten o'clock the next morning. Such a warm, soft winter day in the south of France, students milling about in the streets. Anyway. I picked up my money, two hundred dollars American—*"Tenez, vous êtes vraiment bourré,* " said the teller in a southern accent—and I went out to the docks and sat on a wooden bench. An American aircraft carrier clogged the harbour. It was on its way out, so a student told me, but it appeared not to be moving at all. Just frozen there, like a painting, until I looked away, following the progress of a toddler stumbling and teetering along the boardwalk while his bored mother trailed behind. But then when I looked at the ship again I could see it had moved, maybe an inch or two. For a half-hour or so it was like that, a matter of inches here and there, until one time I looked and by God, it was gone. All of it.

Which is, I suppose, a rather precious way of explaining how that business with the body went, the aftermath. A fitting title, that: *The Aftermath of Donny Most*. But it's true. There were terrible middle-of-the-night pacings; occasions where I was so tense from waiting, from worrying, that if the police had come to the door and taken me away I might have been relieved. Three months later I went into the emergency section of Women's College Hospital with an ulcer. But I remained mum. I didn't crack. I laid off those snoozy pills too and I think that helped a lot. And gradually the distance between the hot insomnias grew and grew, and then I noticed I was thinking about something else first thing in the morning, a lecture, an overdue bill, and then a rather homely student who stayed after class. At least I *thought* she was homely at first, but perhaps that's because she liked me so much. For a number of months I saw her occasionally, until one Saturday night she didn't call to make our usual rendezvous. I ran into her a few days later and when I expressed some unhappiness at the inconvenience of a wasted Saturday night, she was, it seemed to me, in not such a great hurry to mollify me.

"But I'd like to see you tonight," I said, and to my astonishment she replied that she couldn't, she was busy for the next few days. I walked away from the conversation with the eerie conviction that something had changed between us. She left a message on my answering service a day later, complaining about an essay she was doing, the hours in the library, and rounding it off with a cheerful *I miss you*. But she didn't sound sufficiently fractured. I punished her, of course, by not calling back. But she surprised me: she stopped phoning. I waited for two weeks, the phone by the bed, but she still didn't call. And then one night, on my way to the opera, I saw her coming out of a fashionable restaurant with a short young man, stocky, red-haired, in a green raincoat. It was as if I'd been stuck into a wall socket. She was chewing gum, I remember, and, glancing my way, she blew a small pink bubble, popped it professionally with her tongue and disappeared into the back of a taxi. I saw nothing of the opera; I couldn't seem to efface the image of her snapping her gum like that, the autonomy it suggested. So I called her the next day. She sounded happy—but not ecstatic—to hear from me and inquired if I wanted to come over to her apartment that night. Which was not at all our habit because it had always been she who came to my place. But I got dressed up, the pinstriped suit I reserve for Board of Regents' meetings, and after many, many scrutinizings in the mirror I walked the full three miles to her apartment, a bottle of wine in my hand. And how delicious she was, how unhomely she seemed that night.

You're probably wondering about Passion, about what happened to her. Well, there's a story there too. Some six months after our daughter was born, my wife and I took a small vacation. We went to the Caribbean, back to that island I told you about earlier. How lovely it was, to be with her and the baby (a sleeper, thank God), how delightful to go back to the places, even the bookstall in the hotel down the beach, where I'd been so unhappy. It felt like a triumph to return. I promised myself, as one always does when one is happy, to never again take my despair so seriously, but I knew that when it came, nothing would help, it would always seem like the first time.

We came home on a late flight, the baby was fussy, we were both a bit tired, and I may have been a little short with the customs agent, because he sent me into that special room where they go through your luggage.

"Would you unzip your suitcase, sir?"

It seemed to me there was something familiar about the voice. And when I looked up, immaculate in her inspector's uniform, a badge on her breast where once had danced the frills from her bikini, there was Passion.

"Would you open your shaving kit, sir," she said. She shook the shaving cream can, dabbed a little baby powder on her wrist and smelt it expertly. She moved aside some dirty shirts and gave the bottom of the suitcase a tap with her knuckles. Then looking me straight in the eye, without so much as a blink or a pause, she said,

"That's fine, sir." She scribbled a red initial on my landing card and returned it to me. "Show that to the gentleman on the way out."

I did.

Of course you know what I'm saving till the very end. I *did* see Emma once. It was the following winter, a snowy, snowy night. By now my wife and I were separated (eventually we divorced), but being Thursday, it was my turn to pick our daughter up from day-care. It was a cold night, the Christmas lights up, and we were just passing through Chinatown. I was holding her over my head; she was flying through the air in her little red snowsuit, her eyes bright as beads, her cheeks red. "You are so *beautiful*," I said, and she put out her little arms like she was flying, and there, just out of the corner of my eye, I caught sight of Emma Carpenter. She was wearing a black coat and a black tulip hat, and she was standing on the corner waiting for the light to change. I thought to myself, I'll look over in *just* a moment. But suddenly my daughter shrieked with pleasure; she opened her mouth and a little drop of drool spilled out. "Yes," I said to her, "you *are*, you simply are so beautiful I just don't know *what* I'm going to do with you." And then, when I did look over, the air that Emma had occupied was empty. She must have already crossed over. Or gone down the street in the other direction. I can't imagine where she got to.

# AUTHOR'S NOTE

A number of people spent a lot of time helping me with my professor. First, I'd like to thank Prof. John McClelland for sitting still and for guiding me through his days. Thanks also to Prof. Bob Farquharson for an early and perceptive reading. As always I salute Prof. Paul Bouissac for his inimitable style. All three of these men taught me in the late sixties and again in the late nineties.

I want to thank my excellent editor, Anne Collins, for her good taste; Michael Flaxman from the BamBoo, for the extraordinary story he told me over dinner; and Tina Gladstone—for everything else.

Let me express also my gratitude to the ladies of the Gold Hat Health Club (not its real name, naturally) for their patience and inexhaustible sense of humour.

David Gilmour
September 2001, Toronto